TROIS

CAROLYN FAULKNER

Published by Blushing Books
An Imprint of
ABCD Graphics and Design, Inc.
A Virginia Corporation
977 Seminole Trail #233
Charlottesville, VA 22901

Trois
Carolyn Faulkner

EBook ISBN: 978-1-63954-504-9
Print ISBN: 978-1-63954-505-6

Cover Art by ABCD Graphics & Design

Chapter 1

"YOU MISSED A SPOT," Mark pointed out as he made his way around the end of their supersized beds.

Matthew paused for a moment, for which Maddie was eternally grateful, peering carefully down at her already beleaguered backside. It gave her a chance to catch her breath through the tears he had unerringly invoked with that God-awful belt of his.

"Where?" he asked, his big hands paradoxically gentle as they skimmed lightly over her skin trying to find what Mark was talking about. He was not at all convinced that his friend and housemate was right. He always did his level best to make sure that he didn't concentrate all of the inevitable multitude of swats or stripes or strokes she'd earned in one place—unless he wanted to. And, as this wasn't a punishment for a health or safety or other such unbending rule, he would spare her that—this time.

Not that he was going to take it easy on her—ever—but he and his roommate always tried to match the degree of punishment to the degree of crime as best as they could.

She felt, rather than saw, Mark touch her bottom in the

only spot that wasn't already aflame. "Right there," he pointed out.

Having recovered sufficiently enough to find her voice, Maddie tried—unsuccessfully, of course—to turn at the waist enough to swat Mark's hand away and still manage to remain in what Matt would consider to be the correct position, while practically screeching, "Don't *help* him, for God's sake!"

Of course, she missed those big brown fingers by a mile and only received a crisp swat from his ginormous palm on the exact spot he'd been teasing Matt about for her efforts. "You know better than that, Madeleine," he scolded in that tone she absolutely hated—the one that reduced her to a recalcitrant six-year-old as soon as it met her ears.

"*And* you're out of position, young lady," Matt chided in much the same timbre. "I was going to only give you another five or so, but I think twenty's more like it now."

Maddie threw back her head and let loose with a throaty wail at that pronouncement, drumming her feet on the carpet. But she knew that, although the release made her feel somewhat better, no one was going to come to her rescue. Their nearest neighbor was more than a mile away and as her guys had said at the time they found it, that was one of the reasons they'd liked this place—no one was going to hear her scream.

She also knew better than to try to wheedle comfort from the non-participant in this particular comeuppance or any other, for that matter. If either of them decided that she needed a spanking—or hairbrushing or belting or caning or any number of other possible methods of tanning her hide—then the other would support his "brother from another mother" in that decision. They were a disgustingly united front when it came to the implementation of her discipline.

They each knew—as did Maddie, although she would be

loath to admit it, except under the most extreme duress—that neither of them would ever choose to hurt her gratuitously, but rather would only do so when she had clearly broken one of the rules they had set down for her behavior.

But they were wholly dedicated to making sure she toed the lines they had drawn for her. She knew beyond a shadow of a doubt that, if she did break a rule—and there was really no "if" about it—it was only a matter of time before she'd find herself in the position she did currently, although it and the location might vary a bit, depending on the severity of the offense and the preferences of the man who was going to deliver her comeuppance. Somehow, they always found out what she'd done, damn them. She couldn't think of a single time in the years they'd been together that she'd gotten away with anything she'd tried that she'd known full well at the time was eventually going to get her into trouble.

It always did, blast it.

And, when she'd already endured about the same number of strokes that Matt had promised he was now going to deliver on top of what she'd already had, it was almost too much to bear. But she knew she must.

The belt was Matt's favorite implement when she'd done something that he thought deserved more than his hand but less than the cane. He let its doubled over length sing through the air to smack loudly down on that cringing flesh and emblazon new swathes of cherry red across her mottled behind. He ignored her sobs and moans, expertly managing to avoid the kicking feet and landing each stroke true on the rise or underside of her bottom, as well as distributing a few well-placed strokes to the tender backs of her thighs as she howled and kicked in protest but held her place.

Mark, who had just gotten home from putting a full day in at his family's company, of which he had been the CEO since his father had died a few years ago, completely ignored the commotion coming from behind the bedroom door that he had closed upon leaving. When he caught the wonderful garlicky, chicken scent wafting from the oven, he decided to set the table for dinner instead.

Matt stopped, finally, but only after having delivered the exact number of stripes he had promised Maddie—not one more, not one less—leaving her sobbing and groaning where he had originally positioned her over the end of the bed to put the belt back where it lived on the nail over their bed that he and Mark had installed—much to Maddie's very real dismay—the first night they had all slept in this house.

Then he reached down and pulled her up onto the pillows and into his arms, holding her as gently and lovingly as he could, letting all of those primitive, protective feelings nearly overwhelm him as he kissed her damp temple and rubbed her back, holding her so tight and close that she stirred from the strength of it.

Although she did her best to wiggle out of his arms, he couldn't quite let her, so she found she had to content herself within them. Not that that was really a bad thing. Both of her men were easy on the eyes, but then she might be just the slightest bit prejudiced.

No, she was a whole helluva lot prejudiced in their favor —about that, anyway.

Matt was the taller of the two, the quietest of the three of them, a thinker and a ponderer who could quote Plato with the best of them and drink nearly anyone—including the two of them combined—under the table while doing it. He was—as both men were—gentlemanly almost to the point of being chauvinistic, overprotective in the extreme when it came to his chosen—or biological—family. He was willing to do just about anything to help someone he cared about, whether that was through thoughtful advice or the lending of his strong back to someone who was moving, or a swift kick in the butt—or the blistering of one particular young lady's posterior.

He knew, though, beyond a shadow of a doubt, that when he cupped Maddie's face in his hands, he held his whole world in them. Not that he was going to let that deep seated love he felt for her keep him from making sure she obeyed the limits he and Mark had set for her—and using the very same hands that held her so gently to thoroughly blister her behind.

She was nude, as he preferred when he punished her, and he found her quite distracting in this state, as always. His lips descended eagerly to claim her dark pink—already peaked—nipples, suckling hard, bringing them to even more swollen and erect points. But other charms soon called to him and he brought his lip to hers, claiming them in no uncertain terms in a long, passionate kiss that ended with him rolling the both of them—very carefully—to one side so that he could tuck her neatly beneath him. A few quick adjustments of his jeans and underwear, and he found himself nestled against her home.

He never failed to wonder—but didn't want to examine any too closely, lest it change somehow—how he could be searing her backside one moment, but in the next, even when her punishment was as bad as it had ever been, completely sure of her body's welcome. He'd searched her eyes countless times as he did again, now, for any sign of reservation or resentment about the fact that he was pressing her very sore red bottom into the bed beneath them, as well as expecting that she wouldn't protest his possession despite what he'd been doing to her seconds before. But Matt had never even the slightest, most fleeting indication of any negative feelings reflected in those black fringed, hazel orbs.

But he did see—and hear—what he nearly always did when he first entered her, and it nearly drove him over the edge much too early every time when her eyes widened and her breath caught, as if it was always a surprise to her how her body had to accommodate him in very much the same way as she had when they had first gotten together. She was almost unbearably tight around him; he didn't know how she managed to accomplish that, but he was ever thankful.

He stopped, as he often did, with just the barest tip of himself within her, not really even a part of her yet, so that he could watch her face as he took her, see her bite her lip as he pressed forward, forcing her to accept him as she clutched spasmodically at his shoulders—her eyes never leaving his—as she whimpered just a bit, panting and trying to adjust her body beneath him so as to ease his entry. But he wouldn't allow it; big tanned hands reaching down take a hold of her hips to render them motionless, lest he lose control of himself completely as he made himself advance at an excruciatingly slow pace, wanting her to feel every millimeter of his possession.

Which she did. There wasn't any part of her that didn't feel taken by him, most especially her lady parts, which were stretched almost, but not quite, to the point of discomfort. He had rasped himself along every nerve she owned, aided by her own body's generous libations, which only served to help him achieve his goal.

When the tip of him found her natural end, he leaned down to kiss her slowly and gently, saying, "You know, I shouldn't really be doing this now, should I?"

A rhetorical question, at a time like this? When she was completely full of him and pinned beneath him like some conquered slave girl? Sometimes Matt thought entirely too much.

"But then, you know better than to come when you're not supposed to, don't you, Madeleine?"

Not rhetorical—not rhetorical at all. That question—and

his use of her full first name—demanded an answer. The *right* answer, as far as he and Mark were concerned, or she could very well find herself over his lap getting another layer of tremendous swats on top of what she'd already been treated to. That didn't bear thinking of.

"Yes, Sir." Her quick, dutiful answer ended in a guttural moan as he began to move deep within her, withdrawing almost completely before driving himself back into her, not giving her any chance after that long, first pause to adjust to his invasion, but merely taking her for his own pleasure and to exclusively his end.

But he knew as well as she did that she was right there with him every second of the way, even though she was being required to battle her own body's responses to the man she loved, to do the damned near impossible and tamp them down as best she could. There was absolutely nothing she could do, though, about the way he made her moan as he reached down and brought her legs up over those broad shoulders of his, maneuvering her into a much more vulnerable position and opening her up to him even further than she had been before, to say nothing of the fact that her bottom then became just that much more accessible to those roving hands. He liked to reach down all too frequently and squeeze a well warmed, throbbing bottom cheek to remind Maddie of the all too thorough chastisement she had just received.

"No, Matt, please," she whimpered—but knew it would be to no avail even as she said the words—not because he was causing her any distress, but rather because the inherent defenselessness he was requiring of her only served to ratchet her desire to epic proportions.

But she knew there would be none of the usual ecstasy to be found in his arms this time, despite how close she was and how much further towards her own release he would drive her without thought for anything but his own needs.

"Oh, yes, babygirl," he barely ground out, snapping his hips forward and taking her to the hilt in one smooth, invasive motion and causing her to let loose with a reluctant long, low growl as he set every nerve she owned on fire. Having found that deliberately provocative rhythm, he continued to withdraw fully before plunging himself back into her until the very end, when his one last powerful thrust had him growling his completion and reaching down to clutch both full, red globes, holding her tight to him as he continued to thrust strongly for several long moments, emptying himself helplessly within her before collapsing on top of her, barely able to think or move.

At first, both he and Mark were always worried that, because of the vast differences in their sizes, they would end up crushing her to death if they really allowed themselves to relax enough to let her feel their whole weight on top of her.

But Maddie had practically insisted to them that—as long as it wasn't the two of them atop her at once—she absolutely welcomed it. In fact, she practically demanded it, as much as she could, within the constructs of the type of relationship they were in. She thoroughly enjoyed the feeling of a man's weight on her, which was why she had always had a distinct preference for the missionary position, old hat that it was. And eventually, she was able to convince them that they weren't going to kill her if they gave her their full weight, although it had taken a while, since they were both stubborn knot heads, especially when it came to protecting her.

As he covered her completely, his breath huffing in her ear, Maddie stroked his damp back lovingly, easing her legs off those impossibly wide shoulders of his, making him do just what she hadn't wanted him to.

Matt immediately reared up, hair falling into his eyes,

panting out apologetically and made as if to get off her, "Oh, hon, I'm sorry. Let me move."

"No! Stay, please? Just for a few more minutes?" she whispered, her love for him shining in her eyes.

As if he could deny her anything she asked for so sweetly, he gratefully reclaimed his former position and thoroughly enjoyed the feel of her hands and lips soothing him as he came down from the heaven he'd found within her.

They parted long moments later, reluctantly, and he patted her bottom as she wandered in the direction of a shower, then rearranged himself so he was decent. He headed out to the kitchen where the buzzer on the oven had just gone off and Mark was putting dinner on a hot mat on the big round dining room table that had already been almost completely set.

Meanwhile, Maddie turned on their huge shower in the bathroom that was just off the master bedroom—past the walk-through closet that housed all of her considerable wardrobe and acres and acres of shoes—glad, as always, that the guys had insisted on it. It was done in pink marble—which, of course, had been her contribution to that part of the construction of their house, besides insisting that there be a luxurious tub, too, that was big enough for three, of course. The walk-in shower was also more than big enough to accommodate all of them at once, with four shower heads—and all sorts of settings for tired muscles, et cetera—one on each wall, so that it was very much like standing under a waterfall. There was also a bench on one side, which the guys had used on at least one occasion to provide a bit of a steam bath for her when she'd had a particularly bad chest cold.

But this wasn't a long, luxurious shower after a hard day doing medical transcription. It was a much more mundane one. Considering their unusual living arrangements and trying to keep the health and happiness of her men foremost in her mind—at which she didn't always succeed, but she did always try—Maddie did her best to make it a regular practice to shower after she'd made love with either one of them. She never wanted anyone to feel as if they were getting sloppy seconds, so she was always very careful about her personal hygiene, not that either of them had ever complained about such a thing to her. She just wanted to be proactive in that area.

She did, however, as usual after a spanking, only skim the soapy body sponge over her still aching behind. She had forgotten to look at herself in the mirrored wall behind the three sinks, and, for a moment, thought that Mark, who had long since been pushing the idea that they needed the shower to be mirrored, too, might not have a bad idea, but then she came to her senses. Like most women, even though she was a size ten, Maddie considered that her body was too fat here and too skinny there, and she knew she really didn't have any interest in having to be constantly confronted by the image of her own nude body while she showered, especially since she did so more frequently than anyone else in the house.

She was the lone holdout about the mirrors in the shower, and she intended to continue that resistance. But over all, she thought, as she soaped herself up for the last time, the three of them got along almost frighteningly well.

She certainly hadn't envisioned living quite like this when she was growing up, though! She'd never really expected to have one husband, much less two! Sometimes she thought she had died and gone to Heaven, but other times, she would have been hard pressed to identify it as anything other than the purest of hells—but that was always only when she was being punished. She wouldn't give either of them up for, well, for anything or anyone.

Maddie had starting out dating the two of them—along with a few other guys—at around the same time, not knowing that they were best friends. But she had kept everything entirely above-board from the start with all of them, letting everyone know that she was dating other people and that they were perfectly free to do the same.

Unlike the rest of her generation, Maddie didn't sleep around. When she said dating, she meant exactly that. *Not* sleeping together—at least not right away—but going out for dinner and a movie, or to fly a kite, or on a hike. Any man who had a problem with the fact that she wasn't going to put out on their first—or even maybe the tenth—date didn't get a second. She wasn't a virgin, but then again, she also wasn't going to be pressured into anything she didn't want, and she also always let the men she dated know right off her preferences about what was, nowadays, an unusual way to conduct relationships with the opposite sex.

But Maddie had never worried about being different and often bucked the trends in other ways, too. Sex had never become the casual thing that it seemed to be to everyone else. If she got horny, then she had hands that reached, a drawer full of vibrators and KY, and a very vivid imagination. Her sexual satisfaction did *not* depend on sleeping with *anyone*.

Matt and Mark were the two who stuck around, despite the fact that they were going to go home alone at night until she decided otherwise.

She and Mark had been on a few dates before she began to see Matt, also, and he—unlike a discouraging majority of the men she'd dated lately, but very like his best friend—was fully on board with letting her set the pace of the sexual side of their relationship, although he certainly did let her know he was very interested. He was also almost unfailingly polite and treated her with an old-fashioned respect that Maddie hadn't experienced in a while—if ever. He stood when she entered a room, he opened doors, helped her in and out of the car—which took some getting used to. He treated her like a lady, and she decided she liked it. A lot.

He was also, however, a fellow overachiever. Mark had two undergraduate degrees and a masters and was working on a second masters, even when he was already a vice president in his family's business—a position he hadn't gotten through nepotism at all. His father would never have allowed that. When he was sixteen, he had to apply for a job in their mail room, knowing full well that his last name didn't necessarily mean he was a shoe-in.

As a matter of fact, he had to apply three times before he actually got the job, because other older, more experienced guys had also applied. Not that he hadn't already been working his butt off. His father also didn't believe in paying children to be children. From the time he was about six, he had been given chores that had become progressively more challenging as he grew. The Rutlands—despite their money —didn't have a company to come once a week and groom their extensive lawns. They had a son, and at first, they only had a gas-powered push mower with which—if he wanted any spending money beyond the basics he needed for school lunches—he had to mow the whole grand estate.

His parents had taught him—the hard way—the value of a day's work, and that just because he came from wealth didn't mean he was any better than anyone else.

Mark had thrived on every challenge his old man threw his way, from working his way up in the company from the very bottom, Harvard Business School, which he attended not because his parents donated a building—they didn't— but because his grades had earned him a full boat scholarship.

His mother's influence wasn't missing in his upbringing, either. Unlike most of his friends, his parents had always been very happily married, and despite his tough, no nonsense father, it was truly his mother who ruled the roost, and she had her two children—himself and his younger sister, Rhia—marching right out of the womb. She did her best to help Rhia become as much of a lady as she could and, Mark, as much of a gentleman as was possible. As a result, both of her children had impeccable manners, and through a combination of his mother and his father's input about the opposite sex, he became a very loving, protective— but unmistakably dominant—man.

As she stepped out of the shower, she found the subject of her musings standing right outside, holding out a big, warm, fluffy pink towel.

Chapter 2

SHE PRACTICALLY RAN into the circle of his strong arms, feeling them close tightly around her as he lifted her off her feet for a split second before kissing her temple and gently depositing her back on the floor. She hadn't washed her hair in the shower because doing so too often would dry it out, so he started in at her neck, just under that massive curtain of natural auburn curls, and began briskly but carefully rubbing her dry, paying particular attention to certain very intriguing spots. Mark used the plush towel to dry her breasts in particular, then alternately abraded her nipples with the towel then suckled them, as if earnestly trying to soothe away the ache he had just caused. Maddie was too far gone from Matt's attentions for him to not already reignite that spark of desire that was never far below the surface around either of them as she sighed and brought her hand up to cradle his head to her breast.

But Mark wasn't about to satisfy her yet, and she had been hoping against hope that he might. Instead, he turned her a quarter turn, so that his left arm across her non-existent belly held her in place as he thoroughly dried her back, stopping at the very top of that beautifully rounded rump and changing his rhythm to soft pats instead, in consideration of the condition of her backside.

"What did you do this time, honey?" he asked, with no trace of rancor in his tone. How could he? He knew there were plenty of times that Matt had performed this very same service for her, and he, instead, had been the one who'd had her sobbing and writhing on the bed. Or over the back of the couch. Or his lap. Or any number of other places around their house. And out of it, occasionally.

She really didn't want to admit it but knew she had no choice. "Dropped the f-bomb one too many times, apparently."

There was the subtly chiding "tsk" she hated. It was *almost* worse than the spanking she had taken. Neither of them, though, was ever disapproving of her, just her behavioral choices. They were very careful to distinguish between the two, enough so, that although she might break a rule here and there, she knew beyond a shadow of a doubt that she could never disappoint either of them. But the bad language rule was one that Matt was more lenient about than he was—despite the fact that they did their best to present a united front, so that she wasn't allowed to do something with one of them that she was allowed to do with the other—so he could imagine just how many times she'd used it this afternoon.

"You know better than that. I should give you a second round, just on principle, babygirl." He let go of the towel and it was suddenly just his big hand patting her bottom in warning.

Or was that promise?

"No, you shouldn't!" Maddie shrieked immediately and tried to squirm away, but he wouldn't allow that—they never did. She'd never once succeeded in escaping from either of them. They were much too big for her to overpower, and depressingly quick, too, despite their sizes, and she knew she would probably never be able to wiggle out of either of their embraces—at least not until they were all in a nursing home together. She was four years younger than they were and hoped to be spry enough at that point to sprint—however slowly and arthritically—away. Maybe.

But even then—as now—even if she had been able to twist and writhe her way out, she knew that there was another one of them not very far away who would be only too happy to catch her.

Not looking at all repentant enough for someone whose bottom had just been blistered or who was facing the very real threat of another, she said, "Everything was going wrong while I was fixing dinner—the can opener didn't work, the potatoes were rotten, and I spilled olive oil, that I wasn't even reaching for, all over the floor, and nothing really gets that out of your system like a good, loud '*Fuck!*'...or twelve."

Her impudence in saying the word yet again got her a sound pop to her still very sore—and now damp—rear. She had learned once the hard way that one should never get oneself spanked when one was fresh from the shower. Slightly damp was nowhere near dry enough when it came to the force of an unyielding palm against her backside.

She figured there was a lot more where that came from, but he let her go with just another hard swat, saying, "Get dressed. Dinner's ready, and despite the fiascos, it smells amazing."

Pleasantly surprised at having avoided a second spanking —which was a rarity in this household—she decided he must've missed lunch. Very little else would ever have kept him from spanking her a second time, especially since vulgarity—in any form—was a particular bugaboo of his, and a distinct failing of hers, for which she continued to pay several times weekly, on average, between the two of them policing her language. And her behavior. And her attitude. And her every little thing.

Dinner was a house favorite chicken casserole, with tons of garlic and bay leaves, done in a homemade cream sauce with broccoli, celery, carrots and rice, then baked with a generous layer of cheese on top that bubbled up nicely while cooking.

Of course, Mark, who was the healthiest of the three of them—and that wasn't saying much—added a quick salad he had made to the repast, and they all sat down to eat. They had decided on a round table so that no one was at the head, although, if Maddie had fallen in love with a rectangular table, they would simply have put her at the head, with one of them on either side. That was pretty much how it had worked out anyway, to everyone's satisfaction. She was always the center of their attention—whether that was good or bad for her at any given moment.

It always amazed her how much food they consumed, not that either of them had an ounce of fat on them. Matt's was the most physical job; he was an EMT, and thus did shift work, and as he was a natural night owl, he did the overnight shift from eleven to seven, both because it was his preference, but also because of the tidy differential he collected for working those hours.

And Maddie worked from home, having done her time in various hospitals until she was able to slip into a medical transcriptionist position where she could work on her own time and also make a reasonable salary.

So, when Matt came home, Mark was just getting up, and they often had breakfast together. Maddie would, usually, still be fast asleep. She was somewhere between early bird Mark and night owl Matt, and generally didn't get up until her very male, usually very horny "alarm clock" arrived

—around eight or nine—to shower her up with kisses in places that had her practically orgasming even before she fully awoke.

When Matt finally fell asleep exhaustedly in her arms, Maddie would get up and go to work in the office she maintained at home until he got up. They would have a few hours to themselves before Mark arrived, and then the three of them would have dinner together. Matt would head out about nine-thirty or so, and she and Mark would have some time alone before bed.

It was almost an unwritten rule that they tried to eat breakfast together, but that didn't always work out. They did their level best to make sure they were all present for dinner. Neither of the guys was great at cooking, nor were they afraid of it. They just didn't have to do it very often unless she was sick, because Maddie adored cooking for her men. It worked out that they all ended up in gender specific roles, but that was only because that was what they preferred. Mark—having garnered tons of experience while growing up—did all of their landscaping and yardwork. Matt, on the other hand, did all of their vehicle maintenance and as much repair as he could manage himself before giving up the ghost and admitting that he was going to have to pay someone to do it, grumbling under his breath all the way. He tended to want to squeeze a penny till Lincoln cried.

But then, unlike Mark, Matt had not grown up on the right side of the tracks, and he hadn't grown up on the wrong side of them, either. As far as he could tell, from the perspective of being thirty something, you couldn't even *see* the tracks from where he had lived as a boy. His mother was the only parent he knew, if you could call her that, and he'd never laid eyes on his father. He had two younger siblings, and he'd gotten himself—and them—through high school pretty much single handedly—no thanks to either of his parents—and had put the younger two through college, too, along with various scholarships they'd earned along the way.

He'd never much liked the formality of school. He read the classics—as well as more casual fare—voraciously from a young age, but he balked at being told what to read. He was more of a hermit, who preferred his own company and was somewhat shy around strangers, although he had one very close friend through all of his years of school and beyond and that was Mark. Despite the overwhelming differences in their worlds, the two got on like gangbusters and were unstoppable when they did anything together—sports, the inevitable adolescent fights, and girls.

One thing Matt had known from a young age, though, was that he wanted to be like the men and women who had been called to their ramshackle house all too often because his mother was high on cocaine or meth or just shit-faced drunk and wielding a knife at her children. Cops were frightening, but the emergency medical technicians who arrived to bandage the inevitable wounds were kind and smart and helpful, and he was hooked.

So, he did high school—not as well as he could have if he hadn't had to run a household and work full time while he was doing so, but he'd graduated, despite the odds that were stacked against him or maybe because of them. Having a friend whose father owned a going business in town helped enormously, and after enduring a lot of abominable, low paying jobs, he bowed his stiff-necked pride and went to work for the Rutlands on a schedule that allowed him time for school, family and work, with even a little time left over to play the sports he loved.

Once he graduated, he got into an EMT training class at the local community college and got a job doing the grunt shifts—weekends, holidays and overnights—at the local fire department. He was a trained firefighter, too—everyone in the department was—but his real interest and calling was helping people, and he'd never had a job he loved so much.

He hadn't just stopped at being a basic EMT, though. The state had various levels of abilities that it granted its techs in the field, and he had gradually worked his way through all of them, until he wasn't an EMT any longer but a full-fledged paramedic, and a damned good one at that. Once he graduated from paramedic training, he got a lofty raise and a choice of shifts, surprising no one who knew him by sticking with the overnights—only nowadays, especially, he had enough seniority that he no longer had to work weekends or holidays unless he wanted to.

Being a triple full time income household, they were doing really well financially. Of course, Mark earned the most of all of them, a fact which the other two never failed to needle him about, which he took with much good grace—for them—and turned it back on his friends by not so subtly suggesting that they were slackers.

When they had first gotten together, their highly unusual relationship was so new that they hadn't really worked the details out yet, so they had a short-term rental of a three-bedroom apartment in a residential area just outside of the city.

But that arrangement didn't set well with them, really. They didn't feel that having three separate bedrooms was quite right for them, so they saved and lived parsimoniously for a while until they had enough money to put down on a plot of land in NH—the land of no sales tax and no income tax—where they decided to build their dream house, one that would take their particular needs and wants into consideration.

Matt had the occasional construction job as a teenager, before Mark practically strong armed him into his family's company, so he took point on finding them a competent contractor and riding herd on him to make sure that things got done the way they wanted them to—kind of like the way he rode Maddie when he knew she didn't want to do something she'd been clearly told by one of them—or both of them, more likely—to do.

Their first night in their new, custom built digs was one to remember. Knowing they had a mortgage—albeit a small one, considering the size of their down payment—to shoulder, and that there were leaner times ahead because they were going to be making triple payments on it monthly, as they all wanted to get it paid off as fast as they could—they blew out all the stops for that one night.

Both men were in tuxes—Mark, of course, owned his own, and although he and Matt were built a lot alike, they weren't close enough that Matt could just wear one of Mark's tuxes, so they rented him the nicest one they could find for the occasion.

Maddie hadn't let either of them see the dress she was going to wear that night; in fact, she didn't even bring it home—for fear the two of them would snoop in her closet—until the day they moved in.

The only things that were set up in the house were the dining room table and the bed in the bedroom, which the guys had put together themselves, first thing. They were surrounded by boxes, bags, and totes full of crap from the apartment, but it didn't matter to any of them.

Maddie had her hair done just an hour or so before, and she had kept her makeup case and perfumes and things she knew she'd need for this night out of all the moving chaos. Matt had done something special in regards to their bedroom—which was truly enormous, but big enough for all of them to be together in one room—that he refused to let the others see, so that door was locked. She had ended up getting ready in one of the two spare bedrooms, and as she tried to see all of herself in a small hand mirror, brushing the occasional wrinkle out of the satin fabric, she figured she looked about as presentable as she was going to get.

Her hair was upswept, with tiny little Swarovski crystal pins scattered throughout it. She hadn't trusted the beautician there to do her makeup, and knowing that the guys preferred her to look as natural as possible, all she used was a bit of blush on her cheekbones, a very soft, subtle nude and pink for her eyes and a pale, pearly pink for her lips. Luckily, she had a ton of sooty lashes that also accented her eyes and skin like porcelain so it didn't need much in the way of traditional makeup.

A pair of beautiful rubies surrounded by small diamonds hung from her ears—a gift from Mark, while a matching bracelet encircled her left wrist, which was from Matt. A teardrop pendant with a good-sized ruby hung from a fine gold chain, nestling provocatively just above her breasts, completing the set, which was from both of them. All three gifts had been a part of her Christmas presents last year.

She was, admittedly, a very spoiled girl. But then, she paid for it dearly in other ways.

Her dress was a deep red satin that brought out the color of the rubies she wore, and both of them gasped when she came out of the bedroom.

She took each of their proffered arms and allowed them to guide her to the table, which was set with their good Wedgewood china, which had been a gift from Mark's father, along with a set of Reed and Barton silverware. The Cristal champagne was already poured, and Mark handed her a glass, then raised his own to match theirs. As the closest thing to a poet there was in the group, he said, joined by his companions, "To the good things that come in threes."

They laughed, and Matt said, in his inimitable fashion, "And now everyone owes everyone else a beer."

Maddie snorted. "Thanks, but no thanks. I'll take cham-pagne, thank you." She took a big sip from her glass, then allowed the two men to pull out her chair and sat down.

Their dinner had been catered by the best restaurant in town, La Maison. They didn't really do catering, but Matt was friends with the head chef there, whose daughter he had delivered on a call, and the man had been only too happy to make a start at repaying the favor. He had sent over a sous chef with several assistants and two waiters who danced attendance on them all night, through the first course of vichyssoise—which the chef had decided to serve piping hot rather than the traditional cold—through the wild greens with apple, pear, pecans and blue cheese lightly covered by a balsamic dressing, and into the Kobe chateau for three that absolutely melted in the mouth. The delicate slabs of roast were accompanied by tiny candied baby carrots, as well as twice baked potatoes dripping with cheese and applewood smoked bacon.

Maddie thought they were going to have to use a forklift to get her off her chair, she had eaten so much, and they hadn't even seen the dessert yet, which was a deconstructed Almond Joy, with coconut ice cream laced with toasted coconut shavings, smothered in a Belgian chocolate almond fudge sauce and then buried under a seat of Chantilly cream.

The waiter served it in a huge bowl, then provided each of them with a spoon. When they were done—as full as they had been—there wasn't a morsel left. Matt and Mark both left her—reluctantly—to see the staff in the kitchen and send them on their way with their fervent compliments, after giving them what Maddie fervently hoped was a massive tip for their troubles. Then, alone, the three of them lingered over Irish coffee for a long while, talking and laughing, until dinner had settled some.

The two men pushed back their chairs and appeared at either side of her, each with an arm out. She gratefully accepted their help in getting up and was quite sure she was waddling with them to the closed bedroom door. She was encouraged to be the one who opened it, and it would be the first time they had seen the inside of it since Matt had taken control of the problem of how all three of them could fit in a bed together.

As she slowly pushed it open, she could see that the elaborate ceiling fan she had chosen was quiet—the lights weren't even on. Instead, Matt had surrounded their enormous bed —which was the only piece of furniture in there currently— with delicate wrought iron stands of varying heights, each holding a lit rose scented pillar candle. They polished hardwood floors gleamed in the candle light as they all followed a path of pink rose petals to the end of the beds, which were also strewn with rose petals.

It was a truly massive sight. Matt explained, "I started thinking that we should each have our own bed, but that they should be held together, somehow. So, since she's the smallest of us, I gave Maddie a queen-sized bed, then each of us king sized, on either side of her, and I used the headboard— which, since we all read a lot and like to have our stuff around us, I made a bookcase headboard. All three frames are attached to it, and I made sure all three beds are level with each other, so there's no rolling down or up for Maddie —just across to either of us. She really shouldn't be able to tell much that there's a difference between one bed and another, hopefully."

Maddie and Mark were just amazed at what he had come up with and been able to accomplish in the relatively short time from when the house had been finished until they were now moving into it. Maddie especially appreciated the candles and the roses, full bouquets of which were held aloft on some of the pillars, so that she was literally surrounded by roses and candlelight.

She surprised the two of them by quickly ducking into the bathroom, where she had her own surprise for them. It only took her a very short while to don what she had and touch up her make up a bit, then she opened the door to their master bathroom suite and watched their jaws drop.

Maddie had made a visit to a high-end lingerie shop in their area and was very happy with the results. And apparently, they were, too. She had donned a long, diaphanous lacy pink gown that had peek-a-boo panels at some very strategic spots. It was split down the middle from just under her generous breasts, allowing them glimpses of her beautiful legs as she walked towards the two of them, wrapping an arm around each thick neck until they bent and kissed her on the cheek first, then Matt couldn't resist pulling her into his arms to claim her mouth more fully.

She felt, rather than saw, Mark tap Matt on the shoulder, and he—reluctantly—let her go. One of Mark's big hands cupped the back of her head as he plundered her mouth, the two of them leaving her breathless when she was finally released to stand between them, and somehow, one or the other of them had managed to slip the gown's narrow, lacy straps halfway down her arms, trapping them there against her body, her bare breasts consumed by two very greedy pairs of male eyes.

Mark nodded at Matt, then Matt nodded back, and the next thing she knew, the two of them were on their knees in front of her, with Mark holding what was unmistakably a ring box and Matt reaching out to open it.

Chapter 3

INSIDE WAS the biggest diamond she had ever seen, with a good-sized ruby on either side.

And then they said, together, "Madeleine Hope Cunningham, will you marry us?"

She was shocked and couldn't say anything for a long moment. They had talked about her marrying one or the other of them. As the woman who cohabitated with him, she was already covered by Matt's health insurance, which, surprisingly, was better than Mark's. Although they knew she couldn't marry both of them without running afoul of bigamy laws, they had talked about having a civil ceremony down at city hall, so that she would be formally married to one of them in the eyes of the law, then having what they would consider a *real* ceremony—of their own creation—for the three of them at another time.

"We bought it together," Matt said softly, slipping her arm out of captivity so that she could put her hand over her mouth. She was crying, soft, silent tears that fell unheeded onto her breasts. "You're the diamond, and we're just the rubies on the side."

"What he said," Mark echoed vehemently, making all of them laugh. "We'll work out the details later about who marries who, but we both love you more than we can ever say. You're everything that's good in our lives, and we want you to always be with us."

Maddie threw herself into two pairs of waiting arms and they indulged in a group hug, then she hugged each of them individually, once Mark freed her other arm, leaving her nude from the waist up, which both of them appreciated.

Finally, Matt set her a bit away so that she was standing between them, with him in front of her and Mark behind her, saying softly but firmly, "Stand still. We want to get a good look how gorgeous you are in that gown." Then he looked over her head at Mark, and they both knelt again as they each reached beneath the hem and found her bare feet. They began to trail their fingertips up her legs, one in the front and one in the back, allowing the ultra-feminine gown to pool at their tanned, thick wrists until they met their ultimate goal at her hips, surprised to find there was yet another layer of clothing preventing them from possessing her completely.

"What is this?" Mark asked.

"Weeeellllll," Maddie drawled, teasing. "I know how much you two enjoy unwrapping presents."

She could hear two very masculine growls at that and was barely able to save the gown from being ripped off her body as, seconds later, they found what she had been hiding under there as the last impediment to being completely nude in front of them—a ruffled satin and fishnet thong, with a big bow right at the small of her back. When Mark "mmm-mm'd" appreciatively at the way her backside was decorated, she found herself turned by sure hands so that Matt could fully appreciate the sight of her wondrously curvaceous backside topped by a white satin bow.

As beautiful as they found it, though, neither of them hesitated a second in stripping them off her, as Mark forced her legs apart so that he could eagerly nuzzle her mons, and Matt began to gently—and not so gently—nip and lick at her perfect front side. They were both very accomplished at their tasks, and as Maddie began to sigh from their attentions, her head rolling back and her legs becoming much less steady, Mark rose up to stand behind her for support, his arms beneath hers. He didn't need to tell her to lean against him; with the sparks that Matt's lips and tongue were creating between her legs, she had no choice but to arch back into her other man's arms, offering up her breasts to his eager and talented fingers and feeling the contrast of his expensive shirt against the delicate skin of her back.

Matt was well out of her reach—arched as she was, almost but not quite painfully—in Mark's arms, and desperately wanting to touch either of them, she reached back to grab at Mark.

He leaned down and whispered in her still ruby and diamond studded ear, chiding, "You know better than that, Madeleine Hope. You know where your hands should be." His voice dropped at least an octave and he asked almost eagerly, in a voice that sent a shiver up her spine, "Or do I need to remind you?"

"No," she pleaded breathlessly, retracting her hands as if they'd touched hot lava to fold them behind her, which only served to force her breasts into further prominence, a happy accident of which Mark took full advantage, hefting a breast in each hand and squeezing them until she squealed, deliberately offsetting the ecstasy his partner in crime was creating as he licked and suckled noisily at her.

But despite Mark's best efforts, Matt's loving and eager ministrations were driving her relentlessly towards an end that she knew, beyond a shadow of a doubt, she wouldn't be allowed for quite some time, regardless of how close he got her to exploding so early in their lovemaking. Her men liked to take their time with her, to indulge themselves in her— especially on a night like this. It wasn't always so languorous —she very often just found herself taken in the middle of the night, and sometimes, she wasn't even sure who it was filling her almost to the point of pain unless he spoke.

She was submissive to the both of them, however, entirely by choice, and—barring illness—was never allowed to deny either of them access to her body. And with the arrangement that Matt had come up with, where they could now all sleep in the same room, she was quite sure that her commitment to that rule would be tested even more regularly than it had been. To reinforce the rule that she must always be available to either of them, aside from a few pieces of lingerie such as what she wore tonight, she was not allowed clothing in any of their beds.

So she found herself turned and they switched positions, with Mark kneeling before her as if she was some sort of a queen who had commanded him to pleasure her with his mouth, but then Matt's broad, lightly hairy chest was right behind her this time as he nuzzled and licked her neck, nibbling her earlobes and pinching and pulling nipples that were already quite sore—not that he took that into consider-ation in the least—and reminding her that instead of being able to command and control the situation, she was the one who was both commanded and very tightly controlled.

At Matt's behest, they moved to the end of the bed, with her butt resting at the very edge, legs splayed over Mark's shoulders to afford him even more access to her intimate treasures while Matt knelt on the bed behind her, turning her head to kiss her as he used his thankfully short fingernails to add bite to the way he was manipulating her nipples.

When she cried out in times like this, while her most

private areas were being plied with both the ultimate in pleasure as well as intermittent bouts of sharp pain, it was hard to tell which of them was inspiring her response. Moans of distress and ecstasy began to sound very much the same very early on.

But they had been together long enough that the men—who were more attuned to her responses than most men were to their significant others'—could read the signs of her impending orgasm with uncanny accuracy, and they used that knowledge to prolong both sides of her experience, sometimes concentrating on one type of sensation exclusively for a while to change things up.

She never knew what was coming next and didn't know if they planned things or gave each other secret signals as they went along, but it always seemed to play out like a well-practiced dance, somehow, with rarely a missed step among them. When they tag teamed her like this, Maddie was barely coherent from the first kiss until they finally allowed her to drift into an exhausted sleep; she was the center of attention for two very sexual men who were intent on stimulating every inch of her, not only for her own gratification—and sometimes not at all for that—but for their own, too.

Neither of them was sexually interested in the other in the least—in fact, it had been an unwritten rule that "their swords must never cross", as Mark had so adeptly put it one night early on in their relationship, when they were still trying to work things out among the three of them. But they had wanted her to know outright that, although they were as close as brothers and had been so forever, they were both completely straight that she would be the only outlet for the two highly sexual men.

That idea'd had her swallowing hard at first, not entirely sure what she had gotten herself into. But it had worked out well, as she had quite active appetites of her own.

Since she was their submissive, however, she also knew—from day one—that she would not be allowed to put either of them off, whenever, wherever, and however they wanted her, and that had led to her being taken in some very unusual locations that she never would have chosen herself.

Suddenly, Matt was no longer at her back, but gently laying her down on the bed before bounding off it to close the bedroom door.

On his way back to where Mark was continuing to avidly love her with his mouth, Matt reached beneath the bed and pulled out two paddles, one of which he placed next to Mark's right hand.

As preoccupied as she was with the fact that she was dangerously close to climaxing and desperately trying not to, Maddie nonetheless didn't miss a trick, and she saw what Matt had in his hand and had given to Mark. "Noooooo! That's not fair! I haven't done anything wrong."

Mark stood at the end of the bed, testing the paddle against his palm as he said with alarming quiet, "Except what you just did—whine about being punished. And use the 'n word'."

Mark was not a fan of being told "no" by anyone, much less his woman. He had wanted to ban her use of it altogether, but Matt pointed out that that was impractical, so he adjusted her rule so that she was not to use it when any of them were making love or she was being chastised. It was one of Maddie's more challenging tenets.

In no time flat, she found herself positioned over her least favorite piece of their furniture— an A-frame built by a friend of theirs to the guys' exacting specifications. It was completely padded—the builder just used a replacement cushion for an outdoor chair—and even had a little extra at the top of the near side, to bring her butt into even further prominence. It was also equipped with padded wrist and ankle restraints—only the guys had made sure that the carpenter had made the leg side of the frame flare out at the bottom, so that her legs were held much more widely apart than her hands, so that she would feel just that much more out of control.

Maddie'd had to bite both her lips and her tongue as they lashed her to it, not wanting to add to the punishment she was already about to receive because she knew that, regardless of how she had reacted to it, she was going to have ended up in the exact same position.

The frame was collapsible, and she had a horrible feeling that it was going to live somewhere in her enormous closet—the guys' stuff was relegated to two much smaller walk ins, and she supposed that made sense, but she knew she didn't want to be rifling through her clothes only to be confronted by this thing. But that *was* better than having it permanently set up in the corner, where she was now, which not only put her in the quintessential place for a submissive female, which they both liked the sound of whether she was being reprimanded or not, but it also gave each of them more than enough room in which to swing their arms and get that good, crisp crack of oak against nicely rounded flesh.

Matt placed his paddle against her backside and said, before her gave her the first swat, "I had something else done to the bedroom—and the bathroom, by the way—that I think we're all going to like. I had them soundproofed. You can scream your head off, Maddie, and even if our best friends were in the living room and we took the bath brush to your behind, you wouldn't be heard."

Maddie was afraid he had come up with something like that, and although every fiber in her being wanted to wail, "Noooooo!" she managed not to, somehow, barely.

She wasn't given any time to dwell on her misfortune, though, because they were busy compounding it. When she was being spanked in tandem like this, they always fell into a depressingly natural—and horridly uncomfortable—rhythm. If, with one of them, she got a smack every two seconds, then, with the both of them, it was more like every second. Her bottom was a bright cherry red in a matter of seconds, and she knew they were just getting started.

"I think this needs to become a weekly thing, don't you, Matt?" Mark asked, not missing a beat. "Even with the two of us hawk eyes keeping very close tabs on our lady, I would be willing to bet there are things she does that she should be spanked for, but isn't."

"I agree."

"I don't!" Maddie cried, but the "don't" turned into a long moan that ended in a sob, which caused it to lose quite a bit of its vehemence.

"Do we need to gag you, Maddie?" Matt asked, stopping to squat by her head.

Dejected, Maddie replied obediently, "No, Sir."

When they resumed, they began to include the vulnerable, tender backsides of her thighs in their diabolical pattern, too, which had her positively howling as each stroke sent a fiery sting through her skin, not just where the paddles had landed, but all through every inch of her flaming backside.

No amount of wailing or crying would—ever—get them to stop until they had decided she'd had enough or had learned her lesson. This time, it wasn't until she was hoarse from deep, full throated moans and wails.

Mark released her from her bonds and very gently helped her up, only to place her on her knees between them as they both quickly disrobed and she found herself with an impressive, fully engorged cock on either side of her face. She didn't need to be told what to do from there. Maddie leaned to one side and brought Mark into her mouth, swirling her tongue around the head, then taking every bit of him into her mouth that she could, leaving him damp enough that her eager fingers could wrap around him and stroke steadily, while she gave Matt the same treatment, until she had each hand full of them, continuing to slide them slowly but steadily all the way down, then back up and around the very tip, treating each of them alternately to the feel of her mouth in between, trying to make sure neither of them felt left out.

She knew she was succeeding when each of them threw their heads back and growled low at almost exactly the same time, so much so that Matt reached down to tug her up, as if he knew that neither one of them could stand much more of that, and they apparently had something else in mind for her. Maddie knew what it was as soon as Matt arranged her so that she was standing in front of him, reaching down to lift her with one arm—the showoff—to let her wrap those nimble legs of hers around his waist, although he didn't allow her to take him inside her until he was ready, and that involved a lot of deep, tongue filled kisses that left the both of them panting.

Mark was doing his part, too, watching and waiting, each hand full almost to overflowing with a breast as soon as the two leaned a bit away from each other and he could see that Matt was going to make his move. Just as he knew she was being slowly impaled—partly by gravity but with assistance from Matt's big hands holding her hips so that she couldn't avoid his slow possession—he began to pluck at those aching nipples again, abrading them with his fingernails and the calluses she had been surprised—at first—to find a white-collar man such as he possessed, the combination of which had her practically growling in frustration.

But he knew Matt had her well under control. He was of the same mind, preferring to draw out as long as possible that first long stroke, forcing her to feel every millimeter of it as her body made way for him, like it or not.

But they both knew that was *exactly* what she liked.

Once he had her to the hilt, Matt reached out and brought Maddie's lips to his, holding her there, his hands firmly claiming the seared flesh of her bottom, using her own weight and position to naturally separate her cheeks as Mark made himself ready, slathering a coat of lube onto his own member, then finding his position easily with Matt's casual assistance.

She seemed surprised at that, somehow, as his broad head rested against her bottom flower, although she must've known where this was going. It wasn't as if they hadn't done this before, albeit not that often.

Matt continued to kiss Maddie deeply as Mark pressed himself inside her, his breath sizzling in through his teeth at the tightness he found there every time, which was why it wasn't something he insisted on much. He liked that she had to submit to him—really, consciously submit—each and every time. She had to relax for him, open herself to him, every time. There was nothing else she could do.

And he knew it wasn't easy, especially as full as she already was of Matt, yet she had never balked. Regardless, Matt held her more tightly now than he had before, just in case. They both loved to hear her short, sharp breaths, the occasional groan as she was completely possessed, front and back, quite literally trapped between the two of them.

And he didn't make it easy on her, didn't just go in part way just to be inside her a bit. He pressed himself within her to the hilt, making her whimper and moan as those last few inches settled deep inside her and the girth of him allowed her no relief at all from the feeling and pressure of being so widely stretched around him. Around the both of them.

And then, just when they had both snugged themselves as far as they could into her, she heard them both whisper, with the same command tone in their voices, "Put your legs down."

She didn't want to. It was too much. She ended up essentially pinned by their cocks, hanging from them, except for what little support their bodies gave her as they fucked her. She would be surrendering all control to them, buffeted mercilessly back and forth, and what was almost worse was that the position forced Matt's penis to drag against her clit every time he moved. And she didn't even know if she was allowed to come yet.

Apparently, she took entirely too much time, as far as they were concerned, to do as they bade, so they each began to lay crisp, hard swats to her bottom on top of the roasting they had already done with the paddles, making her try to arch up and away from their hands. Not that she could.

She acquiesced to stop the spanking, slowly lowering one leg, with their support, and then the other, until she was—well and truly—pinned between them, hanging, split, from their cocks.

Her guttural moan as she acquiesced completely to their demands—an expression of raging desire and not inconsiderable discomfort—had them each slamming hard into her. Her world was a cacophony of stabbing invasions that she was completely helpless to stop. One minute, her bottom was lifted by Mark's tremendous thrusts, and the next, Matt's uncompromising invasion of her pussy pushed her right back onto Mark's waiting cock—which was something he counted on as he did his level best to withdraw completely from her bottom to await the inevitable rebound that would seat him well within her with no effort on his part at all. Not that he didn't make sure that those last few centimeters were rammed home within her each and every time.

They each reinforced each other's claim on her, by the simple act of taking her themselves.

For her part, besides resisting the inevitable surrender to the sensual input she was being subjected to, she was expected to keep a hand on each of them at all times as Mark nuzzled her neck and turned her head to kiss her in a surprisingly tender fashion as he forced himself up inside her over and over again, while Matt leaned forward to avail himself of her breasts. Forced to arch awkwardly as she was, they presented a tempting target that he would never be able to resist.

He suckled hard, razing those impudently peaked nipples with the edges of his teeth, tugging and holding on as she was thrown to and fro by the near violent actions of their bodies.

During it all, she only uttered one word—the only word she was allowed. She could not ask them to stop. But she could ask for permission to climax with one simple word, terrified the entire time that she was going to do so before they deigned to allow it.

"Pleeeaaasssse!"

If they allowed it, which was by no means assured. Matt, in particular, liked to withhold pleasure from her, both as an exercise in her submission and also as a punishment. Not that he didn't avail himself of everything her body had to offer; he did. He loved to inflict pleasure on her. He teased and tweaked and touched and explored every bit of her, all the while knowing, beyond a shadow of a doubt, that what he was doing had her a hair's breadth from explosion but feeling absolutely no compunction to fulfill her desires.

And he was rapidly swinging Mark over to his side about it, too.

Chapter 4

AND IT WAS Mark who answered her, after a distressingly long time. "Because it's a very special occasion, yes. But don't get used to it, babygirl."

Get used to it? How could any woman get used to *this*? Her entire lower body was sandwiched tightly between them. She was full near to bursting in almost every orifice she owned. Her nipples were being pinched and pulled and rolled and chafed and rudely nipped, but even that couldn't even begin to take the edge off the sheer ecstasy that all of this—even the pain—brought to her.

The three of them were panting in rhythm as she tried to steady herself a bit, using her hands to keep on them to lean one way or the other, but Matt saw that and ordered her to fold her hands behind her back.

She almost whined again at that but caught herself just in the nick of time and did his bidding, which left her even more vulnerable to their potent thrusts.

"Come, baby," Mark ordered firmly.

"Before we rescind your permission," Matt added deviously, a second later.

She didn't say "no" to that, but she did nearly cry because of it. She knew they wouldn't stop until they got what they wanted but that Matt's threat was also very real, at the same time. Either of them could change their mind at any point, and they both knew that the uncertainty only served to ratchet up her desire by creating what they knew she found to be a very pleasurable sense of stress. That sense of urgency, combined with all of the stimulation she was enduring—along with her very deep seated and basic desire to live exactly as she was with them, when almost everything they said or did had a sexual connotation that kept her halfway to orgasm all day, every day, even without any overt help from them—sent her hurtling over the edge, spasming hard around those thick, fleshy invaders, clenching tightly in a way that had her breath sizzling out from between her teeth as she climaxed, bucking and writhing and completely losing her grip on reality. Her men became so excited to see her in the throes of such blatant ecstasy that they lost control of themselves within seconds of each other, pouring themselves out in hard won spasms that had their big bodies shaking and shuddering just like hers.

As always, even in the throes of very violent orgasms, they were infinitely careful of her, making sure she found her own footing and was okay to stand on her own before they let her go, and even then, it wasn't long before she found herself cradled between them on the bed as they all three tried to recover from the reality of what they had all just shared.

But she discovered, that night, after dinner, that although she thought she had avoided a second spanking from Mark for her use of bad language, she wasn't going to escape as cleanly as she had hoped.

When they were finished eating, Mark cleared the table. As Maddie had cooked and he had built the salad, as well as setting and cleaning up the table, it was Matt's job to do the dishes and finish cleaning up the kitchen. And after Maddie cooked, that was a tall order, indeed. She was a great cook, but the kitchen always looked like a bomb had gone off in it when she was done.

That was another of their crusades that had resulted in a ton of spankings. They were trying—with varying degrees of success—to get her to clean things up as she went, because they were the two who ended up trailing after the hurricane that was Maddie in the kitchen.

This time, though, as if sensing something was amiss in the disciplinary force, she tried to get out of her chair to help, but Mark had very sternly told her to stay right where she was—that they had "unfinished business".

That did not sound at all good to her. She was already sitting gingerly on the pillow Matt had put down in consideration of the condition in which he had left her rear end, but she had a feeling things were going to get much worse very quickly. And when Mark walked through the dining room on the way to the bedroom, stopping at the door to turn and crook a finger at her, her heart sank to the polished hardwood floor.

But she knew better than to protest. That would make for a much worse spanking than she figured she was already going to get. So, she obeyed—not that her body language didn't scream her reluctance; it most certainly did. But as long as she responded quickly and didn't drag her feet, there wouldn't be a reason for him to add strokes. She hoped.

Even in a situation like this, he was every bit the gentleman and held the door open for her to precede him into their bedroom. Either that, or he wanted to be able to keep his eye on her at all times, which was a distinct possibility, although Maddie much preferred the first explanation.

Once he closed the door behind him, he reached out and encircled her wrist with his long fingers, sitting down on the side of his bed, which happened to be closest to the door, to position her next to him as he asked rhetorically, "I believe I mentioned that you really needed a second spanking for your use of foul language, didn't I, Madeleine?"

Why was it that deep, stern, warning tone of voice—which they both possessed and used entirely too often when speaking to her—always had her wanting to alternately rub her behind and then her front—even though she knew she was expressly forbidden to follow either of those impulses?

"But—" There was a wealth of pleading in just that one word that she knew from experience would go unanswered. And although she knew it wouldn't do any good, either, she couldn't stop herself from biting her lip anyway, her feet dancing as if she was already over his lap.

He didn't put her there, though. It was a part of her acceptance of her need for discipline that she had to position *herself* there—bottom well raised as a target, feet dangling to one side, hands to the other, inevitably, because she had the bad luck to fall in love with tall men with very long legs.

And when he gathered her wrists in one of his hands at the small of her back and put one leg gently over hers, she was completely trapped. She knew from past experience that no amount of squirming or wiggling would allow her to avoid even one heavy handed swat.

Mark liked to lecture while he delivered a punishment, and he was actively trying to get the more taciturn Matt to join him in that practice. He delivered the same number of strokes as Matt did, but it took him longer because he paused occasionally to say something that he wanted to be sure she heard—or worse, to ask her a question to make sure she wasn't ignoring what he was saying, which wasn't the hardest thing to do. He talked through most of a spanking, but a lot of the time the only thing she could hear was his chastising tone because she was crying or moaning too much—not that that got her any slack in the least, of course.

He felt it helped Maddie to hear the phrases he knew she hated—and loved at the same time—the ones that, said with just the right stern inflection, went directly to her breasts and her pussy, as well as the pit of her stomach, all at the same time, setting her heart racing and her kitty moistening, all while her bottom was being unrelentingly seared by the flat of his hand.

And it was going to be worse than she'd imagined, Maddie found out abruptly from the start as his palm cracked down onto her nates and she realized her skin was still a bit damp from her shower.

"You know better than to use words like that. And this isn't the first time—even just today—that you've found yourself in this position because of it, either. I'm surprised at you."

How he managed to push so many of her buttons at once —without her really even having ever told him explicitly what floated her boat—she didn't know. But he did—they both did, even though Mark was newer at scolding her during a punishment. It seemed to come naturally to them, and Maddie wasn't sure whether that was a good or a bad thing. Parts of her would have voted one way, but others the exact opposite.

She was having an even harder time than usual bearing the pain of the spanking, not that Mark would have adjusted it any, even if he had known. His hand kept rising and falling as it always did, only the discomfort level of each swat was at least doubled.

"Perhaps we're going to have to institute daily spankings —at bedtime, perhaps—to make sure you don't forget your rules like you did today. I'll suggest that to Matt," he said, as if the decision was already made.

If she hadn't been hurting so much, Maddie would have been beside herself anyway from the prospect of enduring a spanking from one of them every single night for the rest of her life, no matter how well behaved she had been, on top of any others she'd had during the day. And the bald truth was that it was a rare day indeed when she wasn't subject to at least one thorough spanking from one or the other of them! It didn't bear thinking of, but she couldn't marshal her thoughts enough while she was already *being* spanked like this to try to think of a way around or out of it.

Who was she kidding? If that's what they decided, then that's what they would do. There were no "ways around" or "out of" anything they decided to do to her. Granted, they both loved her dearly and always tried to do the right thing for her, but since she was already spanked *almost* every day, wasn't that close enough for government work?

"Maddie!"

Damn. She had been so caught up in what he'd said, along with her own pain, that she forgot to listen to what he was saying, and now she was going to catch even worse hell for it.

Suddenly, he let her go completely, and she knew that couldn't be good.

"Go get me your hairbrush."

And it wasn't. They had gifted her with a big, solid wood hairbrush when they all had first gotten together. She had always wanted one like that—for its *intended* purpose—and had naively made the mistake of mentioning it to one of them. Now, not only was it what she was required to use on her hair, but it was also what was frequently wielded on her behind.

She knew better than to drag her feet about obeying, too, so she sprang after it with much more enthusiasm than she was feeling, and then he took it with much more than she wanted him to. He stopped her from assuming her previous position over his lap, and instead, he had decided to position her over the back of her vanity chair, clutching the seat spasmodically as she prayed she wouldn't disgrace herself too badly, but knowing that hope was probably in vain.

Maddie wasn't kept in place by anything but her commitment to submit to Mark, and it was one of the unexpectedly hardest spankings she had ever endured. Her chair wasn't just a bench or a stool, but rather an ornate and elaborate French style arm chair, its legs were much wider apart than if she had been bending over a simple straight backed chair. And because Mark required that she keep her feet as wide apart as the legs of the chair were, parts of her were particularly vulnerable.

Not that he ever disciplined her *there*, he expressly didn't. But just being that exposed was in itself a punishment, of sorts, especially when a heavy wooden implement was being brandished frighteningly close to those tender bits. And, of course, if he decided to spank the inside of her thighs—or much worse—she would just have to endure it—like she was enduring the hairbrushing she was getting right now.

When they first got together, he had somehow sussed out with eerie accuracy that she was a closet submissive, despite the fact that she was very Type A about her job and had risen through the ranks in the billing department until she became the assistant manager—a position she had attained faster than anyone else in the department ever had.

It was the subtle hints he dropped—that later began to sound very familiar when Matt said the very same things to her—as they had gotten to know each other, that had attracted her to him above and beyond the other guys she was dating—except for Matt, who, as Mark often teased him, had come late to the party. The first time she'd actually risked him disciplining her, though, was when she made them late to a retirement dinner for one of the men who had been employed at his company for decades—longer than he had been alive.

He was on time to pick her up, but she wasn't ready, and as she let him in to wait on her, he caught her chin in his hand as the other looped easily around her satin dressing gown covered waist, holding her tight against him while simultaneously shutting the front door behind them.

Mark held her eyes with his, and his voice never deviated from the deep, measured tones she had become accustomed to, but he let her know in no uncertain terms that he found that behavior entirely unacceptable because she'd given him no good excuse for forcing him to cool his heels while she finished getting dressed. If she'd been sick or something had kept her late at work—pretty much anything besides the idea that, as the man, he was somehow *expected* to wait happily for her—he might have let her get away with it with no comment.

That didn't work for him at all, and that was the first time he threatened to put her over his knee.

He'd said it quite deliberately while she was still plastered against him, and he knew there would be no way he wouldn't be able to discern even the most subtle reaction to his statement.

And hers was far from subtle.

He watched her eyes go wide as her breath caught audibly. And for some reason, as he'd noticed with women who were naturally submissive, she also relaxed against him more so than she had been.

Of course, she then immediately switched gears to cover her response, hitting him on the shoulder and telling him she'd like to see him try.

As he swatted her sassy bottom when she walked away from him, he murmured, "That can be arranged," just loudly enough that she couldn't have missed it, causing her to turn back at him with a curious look on her face before she headed back to her bedroom to finish dressing.

Matt hadn't been nearly as reticent about actually laying hands on her. He'd smacked her bottom occasionally—when he thought she was being too big for her britches, he'd told her —from the beginning, as if he'd wanted to let her know right off that he wasn't going to be shy about correcting behavior in her that he thought was unacceptable. But she hadn't actually gotten a full-fledged spanking from him until one day, when they were watching a football game together, which she had agreed to do, she refused to shut off her cell phone during it.

He excused the first call and was polite about asking her to shut it off when the second came in. She got up and went outside to talk, but he wanted time with her—not her and her iPhone. His cell was off—as it always was during a Patriot's game; no one he cared about would dare to call until it was over, anyway—and he expected hers to be, too, just out of respect for the fact that he was actively trying to enjoy the game. She was usually very considerate, and he was surprised that this had become a problem. The third interruption within about ten minutes had him leaning down to press his lips to her ear before she answered it, whispering hoarsely, "Turn your phone off, or the next time it rings during this game—or any other I'm trying to watch—you're going to get your little behind blistered."

Maddie shot off the couch as if he had given her a jolt of electricity, and she brought the phone to the same tingling ear he had used to deliver his startling, sexy, somewhat worrisome threat to answer it as she walked away from him, giving him a considering look as she walked away that he met calmly before returning to his game.

The fourth—and last time—he heard her ring tone—which was the chorus of "Telephone" by Lady Gaga—he took it out of her hands and turned the thing *off*, slipping it into his back pocket.

Her reaction was immediate as she reached for it automatically, easily stymied by his mere size. There was no way she could move him without his consent—unlike the way he could pick her up and hold her against his waist with one arm, dammit. "Gimme my phone back."

He turned that unnaturally familiar gaze on her unexpectedly, the one she knew somehow instinctively meant she was literally inches from going over his lap, and it did make her rethink her behavior as she eased a bit away from him. But apparently, that was nowhere near enough, at this point. "First of all, when the time comes, it's 'May I please have my phone back', not 'gimme'."

Maddie frowned but didn't say anything at that edict.

"Are any of your friends or relatives dying?" he asked quietly, since they were in a commercial break.

"No," she answered truthfully.

"Is something blowing up at work?"

She actually snorted at that. "No one's *at* work. It's Sunday," she said, her inflection indicating that she thought he might be a bit slow since he hadn't already come to that conclusion before asking the question. And later, she was quite sure that her snide tone hadn't helped her cause one bit.

He didn't say anything but used the DVR remote to make sure the game was recording before he reached for the wrist of the hand she still had out—as if she'd expected that he was immediately going to comply with her demand and return her phone—and tugged her over his lap—right where she knew she really didn't want to be with this man. But she really *did* want to be—sort of—although she certainly wasn't going to admit that to him.

Of course, she immediately tried to extract herself from that entirely too vulnerable position, but the heavy arm across her back was ridiculously hard to dislodge, no matter how she exhausted herself trying. Like with Mark, the first time she'd found herself in this situation, she hadn't realized just how much stronger than her he was before she'd poked the tiger. Not that—in either instance—she'd really planned on getting spanked. She hadn't been at all sure that the threats they'd made weren't threats at all, but promises. But she hadn't—in either case—been consciously able to resist pushing them each to the point where the outcome was—as far as they were concerned—inevitable.

They spanked much alike, the two of them—hard and heavy. Matt with just as much resolution as Mark, but just the slightest touch of reluctance, too, as if he hated hurting her, but he knew it was what was best for her.

As the relationship among the three of them had developed over time, he had lost most of that reluctance, but not all of it. As a result, he was sometimes even harsher with her than his friend might have been, simply because he didn't intend to have to repeat the punishment any time soon, whereas Mark seemed to recognize from the beginning that it was one of those deep, dark desires that she couldn't really put a name to, couldn't bear to put into words and that she both truly feared and truly craved. Not in the moment of punishment, of course, but overall in her life, it was something that was sorely missing. He was the one who recognized how deep that well ran, a little more so than Matt.

But even though their relationship was new, and Matt realized he risked losing her for this—or worse—he didn't allow that to temper his actions in the least.

Chapter 5

THAT HUGE, flat palm of his left its fiery red imprint over every inch of her backside, and he didn't even allow her the relative safety of keeping her jeans and panties on. When he'd reached for the waistband of her pants, Maddie had tried to rear up and dislodge his seeking hands, but she wasn't going anywhere until he withdrew that arm.

As a result, she found herself stripped from the waist down in a matter of seconds, and Matt didn't waste any time at all in starting to swat her again. "If you need to be punished, Madeleine Cunningham, then it's always going to be on the bare, as far as I'm concerned. Spanking a clothed bottom is like making love in a raincoat. I want you to feel *every bit* of what I'm doing for you."

She couldn't, at the moment, but she wanted to point out that he wasn't doing anything "for" her, but "to" her. However, there was no way she could accomplish anything other than looking completely repentant from the very first, breathlessly uncomfortable swat. She tried to throw herself off his lap. She even became desperate enough to try to roll *towards* him, but none of her varied escape attempts seemed to faze him in the least. Maddie rapidly began to realize that it was amazingly embarrassing to be held down and smacked, to have it proven to you for long, very painful moments that the person who was punishing you could and would make sure you didn't miss so much as one painful stroke.

When he finally stopped, leaving his hand possessively over her heated flesh, she was bawling like a baby, so much so that she barely realized it was over—although his hand on her bottom made her wary about whether or not it really was.

"Now. Are you going to behave and turn that blasted phone off?"

Maddie wasn't really sure what she wanted to say to that, and she wasn't at all sure she would be able to respond, anyway. She was still hiccoughing sobs and breathing erratically.

Five more swats, delivered rapid fire, convinced her that he wanted her to say *something*.

"Y-yes, Sir," she breathed, amazed at how guttural her voice sounded after all that sobbing and wailing.

Matt tipped her back into his arms, setting her down gingerly on her bare bottom on his lap, but leaving his big hand beneath her. "I like the sound of that, babygirl," he said raggedly, wiggling his fingers playfully.

"Matt!" She wasn't sure whether it was a protestation or an exclamation, and she hoped he didn't ask.

"I liked 'Sir' better," he whispered, kissing her with a gentleness that, a few minutes before, she might have doubted he possessed as he leaned down a bit and trapped her head against his shoulder, kissing her deeply as that hand continued to boldly explore places that brought her a dizzying combination of sensations as it brushed against the thoroughly aggravated flesh of her rump, then delved deep between those warm folds to find the heat and heart of her drowning in her own juices.

She tried to reach down and grab his wrist to drag his hand away from her, not wanting him to have discovered what he already had about her, but there was no recalling that knowledge. He was being thoroughly christened by her body's uncontrollable response to his discipline, and he loved every bit of it. This was further than they had been before; he had been letting her set the pace of the intimate side of their relationship, but he wondered now if what she really wanted wasn't for him to remove her choice about it.

So, he did, proceeding slowly but determinedly, the game now completely forsaken for a much more interesting pursuit, although his point about her obedience to him had been made—at least for now. Matt bore her down onto the big leather couch beneath him, never removing his hand from the very intimate real estate it had claimed, watching her eyes for clues as to how she was responding while he reached up and began to unbutton the shirt she was wearing.

One of Maddie's hands had been trapped between them when she reached for his wrist, and the other was wedged behind her where she had tried to reach back to soothe her beleaguered flesh, so there was nothing she could really do to stop him. He moved very slowly, as if giving her every chance to tell him to back the hell off, although no words like that ever escaped her lips. Instead, she found her eyes locked to his until he splayed the front of her shirt as open as he could, revealing the fact that the bra she was wearing was nothing but frothy, see through lace.

"Damn. I'm glad I didn't know you were wearing that until now, woman," he breathed.

It also had what he recognized as a front hook, which he undid immediately, then slowly peeled back the cups to reveal her generous treasures to his eager eyes for the first time.

"You are the most beautiful woman I've ever seen, Maddie."

That wasn't something men usually said to her. She wasn't model gorgeous. She was too round in some areas and not enough in others, and her hair tended to have a mind of its own, all of which she listed to him before she thanked him somewhat backhandedly for his compliment.

But at the look on Matt's face, hers froze, and she knew she had said the exact *wrong* thing.

"Are you calling me a liar, Madeleine?"

Every nerve was on instant alert. "N-no."

"Then next time just say 'thank you' for the compliment and don't ever try to run yourself down to me again, because you having been spanked five minutes ago is no deterrent to you getting spanked again. Am I making myself clear?"

She bit her lip. "Y-yes, Sir."

He smiled and cupped her cheek. "Good girl."

Maddie was wondering what she'd gotten herself into. Spanked again? She was quite sure she wouldn't have lived through that! Her butt was giving her all sorts of reminders of the painful condition it was in as he pressed her down against the unyielding leather, and she had absolutely no interest in making that situation any worse than it already was.

His hands on her breasts were firm but almost reverent, as were his lips and tongue, and Maddie couldn't stop herself from arching into him. Matt excited her, and her body let him know that in no uncertain terms. He had already begun to trail his fingers up her cleft to find that swollen button, flicking it in an irregular rhythm that kept her completely off kilter. He knew she was already very close to climaxing, but he didn't intend to allow her to reach her pleasure quite that quickly.

Instead, he reached down and adjusted himself out of his jeans and briefs, then took her wrists and pinned one on either side of her head with a hand that supported his weight as he lifted himself a bit away from her, just enough to find a home for the very tip of him, nestled eagerly between those warm, welcoming folds.

As he glided the very barest end of himself up and over her ultra-sensitized clit, watching her head whip back and forth as he did so, Matt whispered, "If you want me to stop, you need to say so right now, or I'm going to take you, Maddie."

Her head stopped mid-turn, and her eyes clung to his, full of unfulfilled desire and just the slightest edges of worry —or was that fear? She was helpless against him, pinned beneath him, inches away from exactly what she wanted—to be fully possessed by him.

"If I say no, you'll stop?" she asked softly.

He gave absolutely no indication of just how damned near impossible that would be for him and replied in a gravelly tone, "Yes."

In answer, she arched up to kiss him deeply, feeling the tenseness in his muscles melt away and maintaining the kiss as he pressed himself into her, spreading her open around him, feeling her body accepting him with a long, low sigh as well as a few tremulous whimpers at his unexpected size.

"Relax," he murmured against her throat.

Maddie didn't feel capable of coherent speech, so she settled for an entirely uncontrollable, "Unnnnnhhhhhhh," that turned into several ragged, hitched breaths as he took her further, allowing her only a few seconds of respite from the tremendous pressure before advancing again, until he knew he had claimed all of her. And then he began to move.

Maddie desperately wanted to hold him, to touch his shoulders or rub his back, but she was helpless to do so, captured and useless as her hands were.

Then came the guttural command, "Lock your legs around my waist, Maddie."

She knew if she did as he asked, she would make herself just that much more vulnerable to him. But she also knew that he wasn't the type to wait patiently for her to decide whether or not she was going to obey him. She sure as heck didn't want to be spanked again, so she did as she was told, only to have him instantly take advantage of how much more open she was, inserting himself inches further than he had been able to before, rubbing himself even more blatantly against her clit, hurtling her towards a completion that seemed much too wild and raw to her, frighteningly so.

"N-no, Matt, I can't—I can't!"

His rhythm never changed as he continued to ride her forcefully, dipping his head to suckle hard at a peaked nipple, nipping a bit harder than he might before soothing her, and saying, "Wait for permission, Maddie. Wait for permission."

That touch of pain took just enough of the edge off her pleasure that allowed her to retain a bare thread of control. She hoped he let her go soon, or it was going to be all over, regardless, and she feared for the condition of her backside if she disobeyed him.

He left her breasts and buried his head next to hers, his mouth at her ear. "I want this, Maddie. I want you beneath me. I want you over my lap getting your fanny tanned. I want to bring you to screaming, fainting climaxes. I want you to submit to me completely, let me bury myself within you and take you in any way I prefer. And I think you want exactly that, too" He drew a deep, haggard breath then said, finally, "Come, Maddie. Come now."

She was completely and thoroughly overwhelmed, so much so that, beyond the screams she emitted right at the peak of her ecstasy, she couldn't say a thing. There wasn't a coherent thought in her head, and she doubted that was going to change any time soon as the violently pleasurable spasms seemed to go on forever, barely lessening at all over time. He had cried out in his own culmination seconds after hers and collapsed down on top of her, then immediately scooted himself off to one side, behind her, spooning her as they both came down from the heavens.

Until Maddie's mind finally kicked in, and she practically jumped out of Matt's arms and began dressing.

He was surprised—and not pleasantly—that she seemed to feel the need to get away from him as quickly as she could. But he didn't try to stop her, either, sitting on the edge of the couch, hunched over until he heard her hand on the door knob. "Maddie."

She didn't know why, but there were tears in her eyes that she knew she had to cover up, lest he decide to come after her. "What?" Was that her voice? She didn't even recognize it as her own.

"I love you."

It wasn't at all what she expected him to say, and because she was so confused about her own feelings, she didn't say a thing back to him. Nothing. Nada. She just left him there, unable to deal with her own emotions at this point, much less his.

She was sure he was never going to speak to her again. What man declares his love to a woman who then walks out on him, regardless of his feelings, and still wants to see her afterwards?

She cried all the way home and knew she really shouldn't

have been driving. She was so distraught that she was very surprised she didn't have an accident before she got home to her apartment. There was a flashing green light on her answering system that reminded her she needed to turn her phone back on, and there were several messages waiting for her there, too, most of which seemed to be from Mark, inviting her to come over to spend the night with him.

Just what she *didn't* need.

Mark was the man she had thought she'd end up with. She'd been dating him the longest, although she hadn't allowed him to make love to her yet. She considered what had happened between herself and Matt to be a terrible personal failure. She should have kept it in her pants. In his pants. Whatever. She should never have let him spank her, but she had to admit to a great curiosity, and frankly had wanted to compare their styles.

She should have known she couldn't do that—on her end or Matt's—without screwing something up.

The worst part of it was that she did love Matt. But she loved Mark, too. She had long since narrowed her choices down to the two of them, not that there had been that many others to begin with, especially once they realized that they weren't getting sex any time soon.

They each knew she was seeing someone else, although not who it was. And as far as Matt was concerned, he had every right to think that, having been intimate with her, she would jettison the other man she was seeing in favor of him. That's how it had always happened when she dated a small handful of men. The field always narrowed down to the guy who got her the best.

Only now, there were two of them.

The fact that she and Mark hadn't been intimate yet was more a matter of bad timing than anything else. She had been incredibly busy at work, and his mother had been in and out of the hospital, and it had gotten hard recently for them to connect. But they both knew it was just a matter of time.

She was so eaten up by guilt about the two of them that she withdrew from the both of them, along with nearly everything and everyone else. All she did for nearly a week was get up, go into work, and come home to cry herself to sleep. They both called, emailed and texted her, but she ignored them for almost three days running.

On the morning of the fourth, a holiday Thursday that they all had off, as it happened, she was rudely awakened by someone trying to beat down her door. Whoever was behind the noise was banging loudly enough to wake the whole freaking building, and she told him exactly that when she opened her door and saw that Mark was standing there, his fist raised to bang again.

"You are in big trouble, young lady," he warned, not bothering to wait for her to invite him in, but brushing past her, hooking an arm around her waist as he did so and hauling her into her bedroom without so much as a by your leave.

He sat down on her bed and pulled her onto his lap, hugging her tightly before saying, "What's going on with you, babygirl? I'd've been here sooner, but you know what kind of a mess my life is right now. What's up with the radio silence, hmmmmm?"

Maddie opened her mouth but couldn't find the words to answer him, especially after he used the same endearment for her that Matt had.

"Maddie." Only one word, but more than enough to put her on alert, and she already knew from past experience that he wasn't the most patient of men.

She was at a distinct disadvantage, too, because she was fresh from bed. She was only wearing a disreputable old t-shirt that barely came down far enough to cover her bum and a pair of panties, her unruly hair scraped back from her face in haste as she sprinted for the door. He was in jeans and a polo shirt, of course. He was almost always better dressed than she was.

Maddie watched in horror as his hooked his thumb into his waistband, the rest of his hand settling on his belt. "Do I need to take this off to make you talk to me, Madeleine?"

In answer, she dissolved into tears, and that was more than Mark could take. Instead of flipping her over his lap, which was what he expected to have to do in order to get an answer out of her, he instead rolled with her, tucking her half beneath him as he held her and rocked them both gently back and forth.

But as he was kissing the tears from her cheeks, he found himself unable to resist the chance to cover her lips with his. He had been more than ready to take her from the moment he arrived in her parking lot—hell, from the first time they'd met—and his desires were definitely getting the better of him, but then he'd always found it unusually hard to control them with her, when he had been able to dampen them at will with every other woman he'd been with.

Mark had been thoroughly intrigued by her from the moment he'd seen her, and her little speech on their first date about not being willing to just sleep with him immediately because that was the current social convention, given with a tense body and voice that indicated to him that she had probably been roundly rejected by a large percentage of the men she had given it to, had him even more so. She was small and feisty, and he liked both of those traits in a woman. He also found he could use words of more than one syllable with her, and intelligence and ambition—of which she had more than enough of both—were incredible turn-ons to him.

They'd been introduced at a fundraising dinner for the hospital at which she worked. His parents' foundation was donating a cancer wing, since that was what had done in three out of his four grandparents. He, of course, had been up on the dais, in his father's stead, while she was way in the back. But it was her table that was the loudest in the place, always exploding with loud, raucous laughter, and she seemed to be the instigator of it every time.

It was one of those rare occasions when both he and Rhia attended the same event, and he leaned over to his sister and asked, "Do you know who that woman in the green dress is?" pointing at Maddie.

"No, but there are lots of folks here who aren't usually. I think the hospital made it mandatory attendance for the whole staff."

Luckily, he did recognize one of the people at the table— Rafe Johnson, with whom he had played football in his younger days. On the pretense of stopping to chat with his old friend, he made sure to swing by the back table the next time he was in that area, as casually as he could manage, of course.

Rafe made introductions, and Mark smiled and shook everyone's hand, thanking them for attending. But when he got to Maddie, he said, instead, "So you're the one who's had everyone in stitches all evening."

She looked shocked, then gave him an impish smile. It was a look he would become very familiar with, in time. "Me?" she asked, trying to play innocent.

But her coworkers wouldn't allow it. They pinned every bit of their misbehavior right where it belonged—on her.

"Some friends you are," she'd complained, trying to look outraged but not quite managing it.

It hadn't taken him long to get her phone number, and he had largely been dancing to her tune ever since, although he doubted she realized it. He had been living in a constant state of arousal since then, and now was no different, despite her tears.

He knew he should have just been holding her, whispering sweet nothings and contenting himself with merely comforting her. But he didn't think he could do it, and it would have been a lot easier if she hadn't been kissing him back as avidly as she was.

Seconds later, she surprised him again by whispering, "Mark, make love to me." Maddie knew it was the absolute wrong thing to do, but she was so turned around in her head that she felt an overwhelming need to be as close to him as she could get.

He smiled down at her and proceeded to do exactly that, very deliberately and carefully, with exquisite attention to detail. He quickly relieved her of her shirt and panties, dropping them to the floor beside the bed, then he settled himself on top of her, still fully clothed. "I like you naked beneath me, Maddie."

Her mouth opened, but nothing came out except a slight startled squeak when he insinuated his roughly jeaned thigh between her bare ones, opening her to him and watching her face the entire time while he did it. He saw a moment of fear that quickly settled into one of passion, which deepened when he boldly began to rub his leg against her privates.

"You like that, don't you, Maddie? It feels good?"

She sighed, her eyes half closed as he continued the movement, reaching down to part her lips so that she had no protection from him when his thigh next met her fevered flesh. "Should I make you come this way? I could, you know."

She didn't doubt it a bit. Hell, all he—or Matt, for that matter—had to do was look at her and she creamed in her pants. She'd never felt this out of control about any man—much less two at once—and it had her frankly worried.

But Mark quickly snapped her attention back to him by reaching beneath her head to find her haphazard ponytail, using it to bring her head up to his, claiming her mouth with his lips and tongue, not allowing her to lean away from him, but holding her head completely still so that his plundering tongue had full access to what it wanted.

A sudden spark came to his mind, and within seconds, she found herself on her knees on her own bed with him standing at the edge behind her, her backside presented to him like a pagan sacrifice to his own desires as he reached down with a hand he'd moistened with his own spit, only to think at the last minute that he should have gone to her for that, first.

And when he, with surprising gentleness, bent down to part her nether lips with one hand and delve between them with the other, he was generously rewarded by her over-flowing libations, which he used not only to slicken his own member, but to probe further, to the top of her cleft, where there should have been a relatively small button of flesh.

But, as a measure of her responsiveness to him, hers was no tiny, reticent presence. She was as fully engorged as he was, the size of a tightly peaked nipple, throbbing and pulsating and almost rising eagerly to his touch while she groaned in something almost akin to pain at his attentions.

"What have we here, Maddie?" he asked, watching the blush rise in her cheeks becomingly. "What were you dreaming of a few minutes ago, hmmmm? Or is all of this for me?"

He stopped and withdrew much too quickly, leaving the area she most wanted him to attend to wholly bereft of direct sensation, making her try to offer herself to him in the lewdest fashion possible, displaying herself for him, hoping to entice him to reclaim the same territory.

Mark, though, was on to something else. He leaned forward, over her, and took firm possession of the end of her ponytail, just before the different lengths of hair began to curl, so he had full power over her head, gently tugging back on it until the line of her neck was nicely arched, which caused her to automatically raise her bottom in response.

Then he reached down and positioned himself against her entrance, gripping the thick hunk of hair tightly as he pressed himself up inside her in one smooth, inexorable motion.

Maddie found herself very neatly trapped, unable by dint of his hold on her ponytail to avoid the pressure of him taking full and complete possession of her. If she moved too far forward, her hair was pulled uncomfortably, and if she pushed back, there was really nowhere to go in that direction that didn't involve her being even further impaled by that impossibly thick, long cock of his.

Not that he was giving her much choice about movement. He kept her on a short leash that was exactly the length of her long auburn curls as he began to plunge deeply within her, being sure to remove himself completely before rudely snapping his hips and claiming her to the hilt each and every time.

But even in the midst of his own quest for culmination, Mark found himself reveling in the tiny sounds she made as he took her, a whimper here, and a sharply caught breath there. Mid-stroke, he decided to bend over her a bit more, carefully turning her head and pressing her right cheek into the mattress, taking a hold of the knot of fabric that gathered her hair instead of the hair itself to hold her where he wanted her, bottom offered up even more generously to him as she was forced to grant him even further access to her body.

"Keep your head down," he warned, not taking his hand off the back of her head as he nudged her knees open even further to accommodate both of his legs between them. "Put your arms straight out and keep them that way until I tell you not to."

She complied immediately, her hands clutching desperately at the fitted sheet, finding no succor there, no relief from his repeated invasion, especially as he made it a thousand times worse by reaching around the front of her with his free hand and finding—unerringly—her drenched little bud.

"Ahh," he sighed as he slid once again into the very depths of her, "you like this, don't you, Maddie? You enjoy being controlled."

She wanted to protest, she wanted to scream "NO!" at him, but she knew it would ring very hollow as he rubbed the barest tips of his second and third fingers over her clit, not even having to move them much as his own act of riding her provided enough motion to drag them with acute pleasure over and over her most sensitive spot.

"You may come, Maddie, but do it quickly, before I do, or I swear I'll paddle your behind when I'm through."

She was flying into the abyss, she knew, but it was the only place she truly wanted to go, the only place she was being permitted to go—headlong, rushing, no chance to breathe or think or protest or even to acquiesce to his demands before his body forced hers into the sun, leaving his fingers right where they had been, pulling every ounce of paradise from her as he rode her to his own almost violent conclusion.

In the aftermath of such a violent storm, she couldn't move. It was just plain beyond her.

Mark rose first, bringing back a warm, moist towel, with which he cleansed them both—her first, or course, and much more tenderly than himself, before pulling her into his arms to rest her head on his chest. But instead of encouraging her to snuggle in next to him, his actions seemed to have the exact opposite effect, and she got out of bed to shrug into real clothes—well, as close as she felt she could to real clothes. Jeans and a t-shirt were the order of the day, as far as she was concerned.

Chapter 6

MADDIE WAS LOOKING ENTIRELY TOO sad for him to bear, especially for someone who had just been brought off like a rocket, so he rearranged himself into some semblance of order and followed her out, reluctantly, to the small dining room as she located, then began to peel a grapefruit as if it was an orange.

"I don't think I have anything to offer you for breakfast."

She sounded alarmingly depressed, and he shouldered himself away from the wall he'd been leaning against, moving towards her as her door began to rattle violently for the second time that morning. Unfortunately, she had no illusions as to who it was this time.

It seemed her nightmare was coming true before her eyes. They were here, the both of them at the same time, dwarfing her between them in the small living room of her own, tiny home, glowering at each other over her head. She made a mental note next time to fall in love with a much smaller man—or was that much smaller *men* now?

"What is he doing here?" Mark asked, surprised to see his

best friend—with whom he hadn't connected in a while—standing in front of him.

"I could ask you the same question, Mark."

Maddie was surprised. They didn't seem to be strangers, exactly. "Do you two know each other?"

"Since kindergarten," Matt supplied, not taking his eyes off of Mark.

"He's my best friend," Mark admitted, staring right back, not that that reduced the tension that filled the air one bit.

They were each fidgeting noticeably, balancing on the balls of their feet, as if readying themselves to either launch or repel an attack.

But Maddie had already had enough macho posturing for one morning, and now, knowing how close they were, she just felt that much guiltier for coming between them—literally and figuratively. So, she put a hand on the middle of each of their chests, as if she felt she could stop them single handedly if they decided to fight, and said, "I want both of you to stand down. Now. Immediately."

There was no relaxation of any of the muscles beneath her small hand whatsoever. So much for that.

She drew a deep breath and tried again. "I'm so sorry that I got involved with the both of you at the same time. I will not be the cause of any kind of bad blood between the two of you. It would kill me to see either of you hurt. And since I'm the source of agitation, I'm going to remove myself from both of your realms." She reached up and brought the both of their faces down to her level so that she could kiss each cheek, whispering, "I love you both," before she turned and headed back to her bedroom. She wanted nothing more than to bury herself beneath the covers for a few days…a week…a month or two. She'd see how it went.

Of course, neither one of them was going to stand for any part of that—not her leaving them in the middle of their situation, nor hiding out for days on end again. So, she ended up having each of them loop an arm under hers, lift her off the feet in the act of walking, so that her feet continued to move mid-air, until they had set her down on the sofa between them.

"Where do you think you're going?" Mark asked.

Matt seconded, adding, "We've got to work this out amicably, so you're staying right here while we do."

Maddie sighed. "I think my solution is the best. If you guys have been great friends since Noah was a pup until I came along, then the obvious solution is the best. Take me out of the equation, and you two can continue to be friends."

"But you said that you loved us," Matt pointed out.

"What difference does that make?"

"A lot," they answered vehemently, in unison, glaring at each other for having done so.

"No, I can't see that it does." She made as if to get up but found herself held firmly down by not one, but two, sets of entirely too muscular arms.

Mark gestured towards Matt with his head. "When did you start to date her?"

Matt gave him the date.

"I knew her before that, so she's mine."

Maddie frowned fiercely at that and opened her mouth to complain, but she was completely overshadowed by the men, who were rapidly getting more and more aggressive about who's she was. "When did you first make love to her?" Matt countered.

"This morning."

On hearing that, Matt couldn't quite find it in himself to crow, knowing she had spent the better part of the morning in the other man's arms, even though he had been the first to know her in the biblical sense.

"When did you first spank her?" Mark asked, knowing he had to have been the first.

Matt looked surprised. "You spank her, too?"

"When she needs it, which seems to be considerably often."

"Hey, I resemble that remark!" she cried, hitting each of them hard on the shoulder, not that either of them seemed to notice. It was probably no more annoying to either of them than a mosquito bite, she realized. There were entirely too many layers of muscle—in their arms *and* their heads, apparently.

Maddie tried to get up again but didn't make it any further than she had before.

"What did I say?" each of them asked her expectantly.

"You're going to get your fanny tanned for disobedience if you keep this up, Maddie." The two of them came up with variations of that threat at the same time, then just sat and glared at each other.

It was Mark who was more of the peacemaker when he asked, "Why can't you continue to date the two of us?"

Maddie collapsed back against the sofa cushions. "I guess I could, but I don't usually do that. I don't know if I could handle it This is a total fluke, finding two men I'm so—" She suddenly became aware of just how much she was going to be giving away, but then thought what the hell. "—so attracted to. You each get me on a very deep level. Believe it or not, I don't find that very often, and I like you both a lot, on top of that. I'm attracted to the both of you and have come to love each of you." Her eyes watered until she got herself better under control and, clearing her throat, she went on, "And that's not something I say lightly to anyone. So, I didn't want to lose either of you." She sighed heavily. "But now, I'm not going to have either of you."

"Stop that," Matt said, tipping her face towards him.

"Occasionally, the old man here has a reasonably good idea. There's no reason why you can't date the two of us."

"Hell yes, there is!" she yelled. "I can't possibly handle the both of you. You're much too alpha for that—and for me. To say nothing of the fact that my poor butt would be permanently reddened."

Again, they both answered, "So?" at the same time.

"Where's the bad?" Mark asked, and he got another smack because of it. "Well, I'm just saying that you're, well, a handful for any guy—not that either of us couldn't handle you. But with two guys riding herd on you, there's very little you'll get away with, which is just what you need, as much as you're loath to admit it."

"And two guys mean lots of loving," Matt reminded her, pressing his lips to hers for a short moment.

"Yes, but then there are inevitably going to be conflicts—scheduling, being together on holidays, birthdays, stuff like that. And aren't you guys going to be deathly jealous of each other, like you were a few minutes ago?"

"Well, we might have to coordinate on some stuff," Matt agreed slowly. "But our daily schedules are wonderfully complimentary to keeping us kind of separate. You're going to work from home, aren't you?"

Maddie nodded, but Mark was left in the dark, asking, "She is?" He turned to her, looking a bit wounded. "How come you didn't tell me about that?"

"I just hadn't gotten the chance, and it's not a sure thing at all. My boss has to sign off on me telecommuting."

Matt added, "So she'll be home all day, and I'm home most of the day, once I get up. You can have her when you get home from work. And we can share her on the weekends and alternate holidays."

Maddie was frowning. "This sounds a lot like my parents'

shared custody agreement, guys, and that is *not* a compliment."

"And as to jealousy, I think that will still be there to some extent, but the fact that we're longtime friends will help that, and I'd rather share you with a man I know and trust than to risk losing you completely to some guy I don't know anything about."

She tried again to get up and was surprised when they finally let her. She put her hands in the air as if she was surrendering. "I'm not necessarily on board with this at all, gentleman. All I want to do right now is go cry myself to sleep."

They were both up and next to her in a shot, trying unsuccessfully to hug her at the same time, which was probably hilarious, but at the time, Maddie was too stressed to laugh about it, and she just kind of checked out.

Mark noticed that and tilted his head towards her while catching Matt's eyes. "Why don't we let you get some rest and think about it. But don't try to hide out, though, or we'll both beat down your door again, and then you'll have the two of us trying to take you over our knees at the same time." He looked over at Matt. "We're gonna go somewhere and talk and see if we can't work this out between us."

Maddie would have agreed to the use of an atomic weapon if it would have gotten the two of them out of her little house. She was drowning in a sea of testosterone, and it was just about killing her. They each tried to kiss her in the most romantic fashion he could think of, but she was well and truly over it, waving them off instead, as if they were long lost cousins she didn't like very much who had severely overstayed their welcome.

They were back, though, later that day, with a proposal they had ironed out between themselves, kind of splitting her

—or at least her availability—down the middle, along with a set of rules for her to follow that they were both on board with enforcing—a bit too eagerly, as far as she was concerned.

She looked at the proposal on Mark's iPad as she sat in the exact spot she had this morning, between them on the couch, then said, "How about putting something in there about me not getting spanked more than once a day?"

They both looked truly puzzled at that suggestion. "Why?" Matt asked.

Maddie snorted. "Because I don't want to be spanked more than that."

It was their turn to snort. "You, my dear," Mark began, "will be spanked as hard and as often as either of us sees fit."

Matt nodded in perfect agreement. "I trust his judgment in that matter, and he trusts mine."

"But what if I don't trust either one of you?" she asked.

"Too late. You've already given each of us that trust."

"But that was before I knew you were going to gang up on me!"

Matt turned to Mark, asking, mock seriously, "I don't see a problem with her getting multiple spankings a day, do you?"

"Hell, no. As far as I'm concerned, it ought to be a rule that she *does* get spanked two or three times a day."

Mark turned her face towards him. "We each want you as our submissive. There are going to be big demands on you because of that, but there will also be big rewards."

She made the sudden realization that they weren't expecting her to eventually decide between the two of the, but instead, to enter into a permanent relationship with the both of them, which was something she had never considered.

She found herself looking at Matt suddenly as he said, "You told us that you loved us, and we want you to know that we love you, and we'll do our best to make sure that we both provide as stable a relationship as we can. We'll both do our level best to make sure that any jealousies we have will *not* be played out in front of you, and we'll each try to make sure that we arrange things so that we don't have any in the first place, although I think there'll probably be a bit of an adjustment period."

He had said a mouthful there. And when they found themselves getting jealous or a disagreement arose between the two of them—and both situations were surprisingly rare, she was glad to realize—they had originally decided on an old-fashioned way to settle their differences—they boxed at the Y. But Maddie found that much too violent, so then they went to tennis, but racquets were still occasionally thrown and not ducked in time to avoid injury.

So, they decided on karate, in which neither of them had an advantage. They were black belts in record time, but each of them had found that the inherent discipline also helped them to deal with the anger that occasionally—and inevitably, they realized—cropped up because of their unusual situation.

And now, they almost never argued, any of the three of them, but especially the guys. They read each other's minds a lot about her and were so attuned to everything about her that they could predict when she would get her period within a day or two of its arrival.

Of course, none of that helped Maddie in the least, while Mark was decorating her behind with the big solid wood head of her hairbrush as he made her shift and dance as best she could while on her tiptoes, her legs spread awkwardly around the wide legs of the chair, gripping the seat cushion her face was inches from as if it was the secret to stopping the spanking.

"Uh—unhhhhh—mmmm—hahhhhhhh."

He had long since disabused her of her elastic waist shorts and undies. Now he reached beneath her to pull up her shirt to around her neck and remove her bra, then put her arms back in her shirt, but left it bunched up well under her shoulders, so that her bare breasts were revealed. Mark liked to watch them move with each swat, and he knew that being still somewhat covered was somehow even more embarrassing to Maddie than being entirely nude.

A quick check revealed that he was right on target—both sets of her cheeks were blushing equally, but he wasn't anywhere near done with that gorgeous backside of hers. Before he was through, he had decorated the entirety of her rear and all the way down the backs of her thighs to a very angry, almost purple red.

But that wasn't the end of it. Maddie knew as soon as she heard his belt buckle clink that he was making the necessary adjustments to take her from behind, but before he did, he knelt down between her legs and reached up there, to where she least wanted him to touch her but where she was entirely unable to prevent him from going. Although he'd made his point so many times over that she could no longer count, he liked to prove to her that her body loved the punishments she was forced to endure, despite the fact that—given the opportunity—she would protest them long and loud.

And she never disappointed him, despite the fact that he knew she found that part of her body's responses to him—to them—to be humiliating in the extreme.

His fingers poked and prodded none too gently, claiming the most secret parts of her as his, just like Matt would when he got the chance to do the same thing. He cupped her entire mons in his big palm, then let his fingers seek out those two telltale signs she never failed to show him—her dripping little cunny and that fleshy peak of hers that more than echoed the ones on her breasts. "Ahhhh, yes, Maddie. This is what I mean. If you were dry for me even once after a punishment, I could probably be convinced to go much easier on you. But you're not—you never are. This is one of the things you need most." He brought the hairbrush down one last time, making her scream in surprise.

She felt him dip his wick into her embarrassingly moist font, slathering her juices all over himself, but then he moved a bit away from her, and she knew that wasn't what he was after this evening. Her hunch was born out by the feeling of the head of his cock as it pressed against her bottom hole.

Maddie knew better than to arch up in protest, although everything in her wanted to. She knew better than to do that and make it that much harder on herself. She could feel how close he was. She could feel the coarse hair on his legs scraping against her poor, ultra-sensitized rear end and backside and felt him slip just a dab of lube onto her flower, knowing he would use no more than that beyond what her body eagerly and naturally supplied.

As he forced himself inside her, thick and unyielding as he was, he whispered hoarsely, "And this is another of the things you need, too, Maddie. This right here." He emphasized those last three words with sharp thrusts that seated him well within her but not completely. Not until he leaned even more into her, seeking and finding the very limit of her capacity and stretching her beyond it, until there was nothing left of himself with which to penetrate her.

It was always a challenge to her submission—to accommodate him in this way—as her various whimpers and moans attested each and every time he took her bottom, which was why it wasn't something he insisted on very often. He liked that it was something that pointed out her submission to him in the most elemental of ways and challenged her very commitment to it—to him.

Mark stayed there for a good long while, fondling her

sore bottom, reaching beneath her to tweak her nipples, requiring that she accept him without protest for as long as he cared to fondle her, occasionally reaching down to see if the seeping had stopped, but, as always, the amount of her tribute had increased three or four-fold. He used it to tease and titillate her, to squeeze and rub and flick her clit as he began to extract himself fully from her body before less than gently claiming her—to the hilt every time—again.

Maddie's fingers clung to the seat cushion of the chair, her fingers becoming claws around it as he dominated her in this humiliating manner, requiring that she submit her will to his, acquiescing to the demands of his body, letting him use her as he would.

And—as her body had already reassured him—enjoying every single second of it.

But, of course, he didn't allow her completion. He pleasured himself within her and pleased himself by teasing her with her own responses, but when he finally exploded within her, then cleaned the both of them up with tender care, she was just as unfulfilled as she had been when she walked into the room.

Later that night, each of them took her again. Matt called her in to the living room to inspect her beleaguered bottom while she lay over his lap. But then he was unable to resist availing himself of her charms, turning her onto her back on their big couch, taking her quick and hard before he went to work, leaving her seen to with a soft, warm, wet washcloth but telling her she must stay in place—naked, in that wide open, embarrassing position—in case Mark wanted her.

So, she remained there until Mark reappeared from his office, where he had disappeared just after her last punishment—seeing her still nude on the couch, her pussy on complete display the entire time, glistening with more and more of her juices as she did so, while she submitted, lying there, unable to relieve the ache that had been created and left unfulfilled within her multiple times that day.

"Get up, chick," Mark ordered. "Your legs must be sore from that position."

They were, but she barely noticed it for the fire in her bottom and her clit.

"Come to bed."

When Mark said bed, he meant bed. There would be no TV for her, tonight. Luckily, all of her favorite shows had already long since been programmed into the DVR. She would have curled up in his arms on his bed, but when he came to her, he rolled her onto her back and slid into her, his strokes long and slow and designed to draw the pleasure out —his, of course, more so than hers.

Maddie was beside herself, desperately needing that final culmination she knew she would not be experiencing this evening. The only thing she could hope for was a wet dream, but despite the fact that she was deliberately kept in a constant state of very high arousal, she was rarely blessed with one of them. Her dreams were about much less inter-esting things—traffic, shopping, and work, occasionally.

And she was right. Mark cried out when his body clenched within her, and he pumped another few times in and out of her, but then he drew her into his arms, spooned her, kissed her ear and fell asleep within seconds.

Sleep evaded Maddie, though, till nearly dawn. Sexual frustration often did that to her. It was nearly time for Matt to come home before she fell into a deep sleep.

Chapter 7

IN HER DREAM, she found her legs being gently folded up and well back, her wrists already caught in somehow familiar, restrictive but comfortable bonds. She was leaning back against something hard and muscular as big hands roved over her shoulders and down the front of her, massaging here, tweaking there, until each of her breasts was hefted and squeezed like someone meant it, those impudent nipples captured between thumb and forefinger, being pinched and rolled at the same time—just as she liked. Maddie happily settled back to enjoy the rare sex dream, but when the most sensitive spot on her body was trapped within the warm, wet confines of a loving mouth that began to flick her clit with the hard point of a tongue, she realized that this was *not* a dream.

Although she had awakened, she was not able to open her eyes and began to panic a bit because of it.

Matt leaned down and "shhh'd" her quietly. "You're safe and very loved, Maddie. Just submit."

There was that word again. They both loved using it to remind her that, once she had accepted the premise that she was going to try to handle being involved with the two of them at the same time. Mark, who had seen a deeper need in her than just to be spanked, had brought them together one night at his place, and after a wonderful dinner of phenomenal food—catered, so that he could spend more time with them—and tons of laughter, they both guided her into his bedroom to sit down on the end of the bed and begin undressing her, with her standing between them like some life-sized dress up doll. Every time she made a negative comment or tried to resist, she received sharp, hard swats to her behind—only five at first, but they seemed to rise by increments of five each time she did something they didn't like.

Once she was nude—with a pretty but sore behind—they had encouraged her to kneel in front of them.

It was Mark who spoke, although he let her know that he was speaking for the both of them. "Although we feel that your regular discipline is going very well," he began, watching the blush rise up through her body to end in a delicate flush of her cheeks, he continued, "I feel—and Matt agrees—that you would benefit from something a bit deeper than just what might be considered to be domestic discipline."

Maddie looked a bit bewildered and not a little nervous at his statement, her eyes darting back and forth between theirs.

"We want you to submit to us completely," Matt said as he unbuttoned his pants and stepped towards her to present his already nearly erect penis and press it to her lips.

Maddie accepted it eagerly, sliding her mouth down to the base, relaxing the back of her throat to accommodate his length completely, then slipping him slowly, very slowly, out.

"Good," Mark praised. "But when we say completely, we mean just that. You will have no say in anything about yourself—how and where we take you, what clothes you wear, even your job—unless we ask for your input and your feedback is rendered quietly and respectfully. We may find that we don't want to—or it's impractical—to micro-manage some aspects of your life, but that doesn't mean that you wouldn't be expected to acquiesce if we did."

She had to admit she was intrigued. Their arrangement had been working really well—much better than she had expected it to, frankly, despite the fact that she often found herself on the receiving end of two or more spankings in a row, depending on how she had misbehaved recently and what everyone's schedule was.

"You will quit your job—there's no need for you to work when the both of us bring in more than enough money to support you—and stay home, in order to be more available to us whenever we might want you."

That was a surprise and would be a considerable challenge for her. She liked her job, and had been working at something or other since she was twelve or so and got her first taste of being paid for babysitting. And she was in line for her manager's position, eventually.

But she knew Matt, in particular, felt a bit like he got the short end of the stick, since she was at work while he was free during the day, once he'd slept. In a way, that worked for her. If she was at work, she couldn't really be spanked—although that particular fallacy had been disproved to her on a few occasions when one or the other of them had whisked her away for her lunch hour, only to drop her back at the office with a bottom she didn't want to sit down on. At least, the time constraints of their careers cut down on it a bit, anyway.

She opened her mouth, then rethought it, figuring correctly that she hadn't been given leave to speak.

Matt saw her and said, "Let Mark finish," between pants.

In some sort of coordinated move between them, she ended up on the bed, never having been given a chance to stop suckling at Matt's cock, helped onto her knees as Mark joined them behind her. His presence there made her more than a little bit nervous.

He had been dropping hints that he was going to go somewhere where no man had gone before sometime soon, and despite the fact that she found that idea ultimately very thrilling, and the act itself excitingly submissive, she knew how big he was and wasn't at all sure she was going to be able to do that.

"The other big thing we're going to do is move in together. Matt and I have found a three-bedroom apartment that's just about perfect for us. I can leave my place any time at all, because the company owns it, and I know your lease is up shortly, as is Matt's. It's perfect timing. Living together will allow us much more access to you, as well as the ability to monitor and correct your behavior on a more intimate, real-time basis than we can now."

As Maddie relaxed even further, Matt began to pump himself in and out of her mouth a bit more vigorously, at least until she heard the top of the Astroglide container being opened, and felt rather than saw Mark slather a generous amount first on that already cringing spot between her bottom cheeks, then on himself.

But before he expected her to accept his presence within that very private entrance of hers, he dipped his fingers into the lube, too, laying the end of his index finger against her tightly puckered flower and pushing, gently but firmly.

She wanted to protest loudly, but her mouth was otherwise engaged. And her attempts to wiggle away from that invader only garnered her a thoroughly uncomfortable string of stinging swats to her defenseless behind, and his finger was no less present in it, either. She hadn't managed to dislodge him in the least. On the contrary, as he'd cracked his palm down on her silky soft flesh, he'd wiggled it even further into her, right up to the last knuckle. While he continued to pepper her backside with crisp, hard smacks, he withdrew that finger, all the way, only to press it back into her much less carefully than he had the first time, causing her to groan slowly in protest, which was really the only thing she could do about it.

Stopping the action of her mouth on Matt wasn't acceptable, either, she found, when she didn't immediately press her lips back over him and he reached down to viciously pinch each of her nipples, pressing his thumbs and forefingers together mercilessly and tugging down hard. Maddie immediately did what she knew she should have done in the first place, but he didn't let up until she'd gotten well back into the rhythm he preferred, while Mark fucked her bottom with ever increasing strength using that huge finger of his.

Until he withdrew it, finally, only to cross his middle finger over his index finger and begin—not slowly enough at all for her—to lodge them both in her reluctant behind, twisting them slowly back and forth as he advanced them, listening to her carefully for signs of true distress, rather than whimpers and moans that apparently didn't count.

It also probably didn't help that, once he'd seated them fully deep inside her, she let slip with a moan that was nothing but pure, unadulterated pleasure at being so fully stretched and filled.

"Mmmmmm-hmmmmm," Mark exclaimed. "Just as I thought. It's just like the spankings. She wants us to think that she doesn't like it, but it's a sham." He slipped his spare hand up between her legs and found exactly what he wanted to prove his point, presenting slick, wet fingers to Matt over her back. "She loves every second of every bit of this." He placed his fingers, bathed as they were in a combination of her own moisture and lube, right over her clit, rubbing and pinching incessantly, making it immediately hard for her to breath enough to do what she needed to for Matt, and drawing moan after very reluctant moan out of her, especially since he was still rudely thrusting his doubled over fingers in and out of her backside.

Long minutes later, as she battled herself for control of her own orgasm, already knowing she needed permission for that release, they both withdrew to instead position her on her side in the middle of the bed, facing Matt who reached down and tugged her top leg over his hip, letting the head of his cock rest at the opening to her pussy. He held her still against him while Mark lay behind her, using his thumbs to tug her cheeks apart and expose her entrance to his rock-hard cock, which he placed himself against.

Maddie now realized what they intended to do, but it was too late to stop them—not that she could—or protest in any way as the two of them began to press themselves inside her at the same time, each of them filling her very slowly, making her feel entirely vulnerable and submissive to them and completely possessed by them at the same time.

Mark reached around her to capture the nipples that Matt had been worrying a few minutes ago, while Matt kissed her deeply, and neither of them let her go until—long moments later—she found herself doubly penetrated, full near to bursting in both places, the physically closest to the two of them that she would probably ever be as she felt her body spasm around each of them at different times and tried to accommodate them within her.

There was nowhere for her to go for relief from the uncomfortable—and uncomfortably sexual—sensations that were overwhelming her, and she knew she wasn't going to find it from either of them. They just kept squeezing her between them like a pancake, until she was sure they were going to meet in the middle of her, somehow.

As he held himself inside her, plucking at already raw, aching nipples, Mark pressed his mouth to her ear and said, "This is where you belong, Maddie. This is where you need to be—between us, full of us, sore here," he pinched her buds, then reached down to cup a fiery cheek, "and here."

Then they began to move, slowly at first; one, then the other, so that she was always possessed by one of them, their natural body movements each aiding the other's cause as their rhythms built. They switched jurisdictions occasionally, with Matt biting those beleaguered nipples and Mark turning her head so that he could kiss her, if a bit awkwardly. There wasn't a second when she wasn't being wholly stimulated directly, in every place that counted on her body—except her clit, which was sitting up and fairly begging for attention but was being summarily ignored by the men who controlled her completely—now and in the future, it seemed.

When they each reached their end, practically slamming into her before arching themselves even further up inside her at almost the same time, they both groaned as if in great pain, then collapsed, nearly lifeless, as their bodily fluids drained into her.

Afterwards, when they had taken long moments to recover, their concern was wholly for her. Each of them must have asked her twelve times whether she was all right as they guided her into Mark's big shower, seeing her squeaky clean —in all her cracks and crevices before addressing themselves. Matt had left Mark to his own shower as he dried Maddie thoroughly, then led her back to the bed.

"Rest. You've been through a lot tonight."

She really hadn't been trying to obey or disobey, but her body took over and she was asleep in seconds, long before a thoroughly relaxed and slightly damp Mark hauled her into his arms, Matt having already left for work.

Maddie had quickly found that submission was a variable thing on her end. Sometimes, she reveled in every single challenging, thoroughly carnal moment of it and met every test they put her to gladly, although she knew that most of them would end leaving her achingly unfulfilled. Other times, she wanted nothing to do with it—usually just after her period ended, when her hormones were at a low ebb and she would have preferred not to be touched by anyone.

Unfortunately, she had yielded that right when she accepted their dominance of her, although at this moment, she wasn't much interested in stopping either of them, regardless. They appeared bent on her satisfaction, and she intended to happily go along for the ride, her body already weeping in frustration from its many previous, unmet, desires.

Matt, trying to assist Mark in his goal, brought his knees up and looped a leg of hers over each of them, spreading her more fully open for Mark's delectation, which had her practically hanging by her legs between his, her bottom inches from the mattress until her muscles began to stretch and yield to his demand, his fingers on her breasts helping to distract her from the slight discomfort.

Mark was far from lazy while Matt tried to ease his access to her. He had an instrument he'd never used on her before, all lubed up and ready when he leaned a bit away from her and reached for it. Matt's forethought in positioning her this way was a great help to him, because it not only displayed her beautiful pussy quite completely but also allowed him much easier access to that other tightly closed ring of flesh a bit south of there, which was just where he fit the snub nose of the relatively small plug he'd acquired recently. It wasn't the smallest size, but the next one up. He knew that if she could take him—and she did, occasionally, then the smallest size would be no challenge at all for her. This one was shaped like a cock with a girth perhaps the tiniest bit bigger than his, especially at the very end where it widened quite a bit before narrowing starkly, so that it would stay inside her with no help from him once placed there.

When he began to push it up inside her, not harshly, but not all that slowly, either, she began to keen loudly and he stopped immediately. "Am I hurting you?" he asked.

Maddie knew what he was asking. He meant was he seriously hurting or tearing her—causing bodily harm, which neither of them ever wanted to do to her, of course. And although there was a considerable temptation to answer him with an emphatic "*Yes*!", she knew that he'd catch her in the lie—somehow—and she'd be the worse for it.

She panted, trying to relax enough not to tense up at the invasion of that cool, unyielding thing he'd left inside her until he could determine whether or not she was truly in distress, but was only partially successful. "N-nuh- noooooo," she groaned reluctantly, and the advance began again immediately.

"Then what am I going to tell you to do, Madeleine Hope?" Mark asked sternly.

She didn't want to say it. She didn't. Somehow acknowledging it was worse than most things they made her do. "Ahhhh, uhhhhhh, ohhhhhhhh," she squealed as that thick plug was wedged up into her. "Ssssss-submit," she nearly yelled as Mark seated the thing fully, pausing at its widest point to push it slowly into her, making her feel real relief when her muscles closed around the thinner area just before the flange, and she relaxed a little. Until he pressed some sort of button and the thing began to vibrate.

They each knew her much too well, knew exactly what got to her the most. Mark followed the filling of her backside by working two thick fingers—not crossed—into her kitty, stretching it open much less carefully than he had her bottom, his flesh transmitting those relentless sensations inside her there, too, as he settled his mouth back over her now much more distended clit.

Matt nibbled at her neck, knowing how much that drove her crazy, teasing and torturing those impudent tips, and commanding in a deep, throaty whisper, "Arch your back, Maddie."

Doing so only pressed her poor abused breasts even further into his cruel, waiting hands, but she knew she must obey him.

But it wasn't enough. "More," he encouraged, pinching her nipples even harder. "I'm not going to let you come unless you show me you want me to stretch and pinch and make the little nipples hurt bad, Maddie."

She whimpered, but that was her only form of protest as she did her best to comply with his wishes, feeling him greedily claim every inch of her breasts, squeezing tightly, as she contorted herself to offer him even more.

After long seconds of intense discomfort that still knocked back her overarching desire only a bit, he finally breathed, "All right, Maddie, you may come but do it quickly. Do it now."

As happened at times, when she'd had a lot of buildup, the moment she had been reaching for but been denied for so long seemed to elude her as soon as she knew it was okay to let herself go. She was right there—right there! She'd been there for days! But she just couldn't seem to get the extra millimeter she needed to explode.

Until Mark reached down with his spare hand and began to tug the plug out of that clinging ring of flesh, only drawing it out enough so that she had to endure the widest part of it—the bit that stretched her the most—being released very reluctantly, despite the pain it caused, but that was only for him to turn right around and press it back into her, always keeping it right at the edge of having fought its way inside her, then immediately beginning to slide it right back out of her.

That was more than Maddie needed to send her flying, practically fainting with the strength of her orgasm. She bucked and writhed and screamed and moaned, and they accepted it as their due, demanding even more from her as they wrung five very hard orgasms from her unwilling body, using every trick they knew about what she liked to drain every bit of ecstasy from her, until she literally collapsed in a heap.

While she was still trying to come down from such a violent crescendo, Mark extracted himself from between her legs, taking his toys with him, then leaned down to press a warm, loving kiss onto her lips.

"I've got to get to work, babygirl. I'll leave you in Matt's capable hands. You rest today, okay? We'll take care of everything."

Maddie was just far gone enough to absorb the tenor of his speech, although not necessarily the content, not that it mattered that much. Matt cleaned her up with infinite tenderness, then tucked the both of them under the covers, turned on a white noise program on her laptop, and cuddled her in her favorite sleep position, curled against his side, her head on his chest.

She was asleep even before he pressed his lips to her temple to tell her to do just that.

Chapter 8

DESPITE THE FACT that ninety nine percent of her life was taken up by two very demanding men who would be very happy to keep her barefoot at home—if not pregnant—and despite the fact that they thoroughly enjoyed controlling nearly every aspect of her life, they were surprisingly generous about allowing her to go out with her friends, as long as she asked in advance. They'd even allowed Maddie to take short trips with them, but only over a long weekend, no more than four days away from them at a time, and that was only if she had been on her very best behavior. As it was, even when she just stayed overnight with a friend who only lived a couple of hours away, they were inordinately pleased to have her back the next day when she got home.

They wanted her to be happy, and they knew that her friends were a big part of her life before they had all gotten together, so they accommodated her in that direction as much as they could, although there were a few friends of hers they had put their feet down—collectively—about. Anyone who did drugs or was what they considered to be "too wild"—an exact description of which she could never pry out of them—wasn't going to cut it, as far as they were concerned.

Luckily, her friends who met that description were few and far between, more like acquaintances than good friends, since she wasn't really that kind of person herself. Not that her close-knit group of girlfriends didn't get into trouble—and get *her* into trouble, specifically. They most certainly did.

And they all knew about her lifestyle, too—the fact that not only was she submissive and spanked, but she slept with both of the two hunky guys who were disciplining her and was married to one and considered herself just as married to the other.

The only person of any import in their lives who had truly balked at their living arrangements was Mark's sister, who had become more deeply religious than the rest of the family and was not likely to endorse her brother's current situation. But she wasn't nasty about it; she just had—much to Mark's disappointment—distanced herself a bit from him when they all moved in together.

His parents were fine with it, surprisingly. He would really have thought they would have been the ones who objected, but they didn't. With Rhia's withdrawal from the family, Maddie stepped right into his mother's affections, and they had become close. Mark's father was not in good health, and as his health had declined, he had become closer to his son, Maddie was glad to see.

Maddie had lost some friends due to her relationships, but, like the ones Matt and Mark had ruled out, they were fringe friends who proved themselves to be fair weather as well, so she happily let them go.

Her best friend of more years than she liked to calculate, Beanie D'Angelo—a dyed in the wool innocent who had only ever slept with one man, her husband, Jack, in her life—had gone so wide eyed when Maddie had told her that she had worried they'd become stuck that way.

Beanie was the type who had done exactly what she had said she was going to do when they were both in the ninth grade. She married Jack D'Angelo the month after she graduated high school and had been a very happy—if somewhat cloistered—stay at home wife and mother since then, despite the fact that she had graduated third in their class and had been offered several full scholarships that she could have taken advantage of, with absolutely no regrets about her choices whatsoever.

She loved to hear about Maddie's exploits, however, especially since she knew of her friend's particular proclivities and interest and the only sexual flavor she and her husband had ever tried was vanilla. "Not even with a swirl," she'd once lamented, then laughed, because neither of them would really have changed a thing.

They'd been in their favorite haunt—an old hippie, crunchy granola joint that served wonderful salads with unusual greens that Beanie always referred to as lawn clippings, called Clem's. And it didn't hurt that they made their own ice cream, hot fudge sauce, and whipped cream, too, "to balance out the healthy salad," she would always say as she finished her chef's salad made with real turkey breast, their own dressing and garlic butter croutons and ordered a brownie sundae without missing a beat.

She'd forgotten all about the salad, though, as what Maddie had said soaked into her brain. "Wait. Hadn't you narrowed it down to Mark? Wasn't that the whole gist of our last conversation?"

She had tried to help her friend through those dark days when she was truly putting herself through the wringer for being equally as in love with the both of them. There had been several nights when the two of them had stayed up on the phone, or Skyping, and, that first night, she had been so worried about Maddie that she had actually come over, beating on her door much like the guys had a few days later until she got up and let her in.

"It was, but then Matt barged in—a lot like you did, only much more loudly and forcefully—on Veteran's Day and..." She bit her lip, embarrassed to admit this, even to her best friend. "We made love. And although it was amazing and wonderful and all of those good things, it just made me feel worse about it—kind of as if I'd betrayed Mark with him."

She took a long sip of her sweet cinnamon tea and thought for a moment before she continued. "The next thing I knew, guess who else was practically knocking the door off its hinges?"

"Mark?"

Maddie nodded. "Yep. The two of them, practically toe to toe, about ready to tear each other limb from limb over me. How freakin' bizarre is that?"

Beanie knew that her friend had no idea how beautiful she was—inside and out. And it wasn't an act and it wasn't being modest. Beanie knew that, with Maddie, as with a lot of women, when she looked into the mirror, she didn't see gorgeous big eyes ringed with long thick lashes that didn't require mascara at all or creamy, nearly flawless skin, gorgeous hair or a killer figure. She saw every blemish she'd ever had, dark shadows under her eyes, skin so light she thought it made her look like she was some emo kid in makeup, a too big butt and too skinny legs, and if Beanie let her, the list would go on.

"It's not bizarre at all, and you know it, but go on."

Maddie stuck her tongue out at her friend, convinced she was just trying to buck her up. "I didn't know until then that they knew each other and were—are—best friends. Well, anyway, I stood between them, trying to keep them from getting violent." She snorted. "Like me standing there was going to stop anything if they'd really wanted to fight."

"It most certainly would," Beanie corrected once the waitress had taken away their dinner dishes and brought the requisite sundae and two spoons. "If they love you, then they don't want to hurt you," she stated, then corrected as an afterthought, "discipline notwithstanding, or even just upset you."

Beanie frankly thought her friend was crazy to let anyone spank her, but she held her tongue. That was an old argument, one that they'd had to agree to disagree about or it was going to tear apart their friendship, and neither of them wanted that.

"They ended up going away to talk things out and coming back to me to talk about dating them both and, well, it just blossomed from there. Moving in with them was just the next phase, I guess."

Beanie looked stunned. "You mean you're living with *both* of them?"

"Yes. Didn't you get my note on Facebook about my change of address?"

"Yeah, but…" She stared at her friend, as if she didn't quite believe her. "And you're sure they're not, you know, getting it on, on the side, with each other?"

That had been something that a few of her friends—now her ex-friends—had refused to believe—that Matt and Mark weren't involved with each other as well as with her. But Maddie had never seen any evidence to the contrary, although she had been avidly looking for it ever since they had begun this unusual triangle.

"No, they're not. I'd definitely know that. Besides, they

spend almost no time alone with each other. When they're home, they're with me. When would they do it?"

"Where there's a will, etcetera, etcetera, etcetera."

Maddie devoured a spoonful of sinful, creamy, chocolate paradise, saying, "Well, I don't think there's a will to do that in either of them. I mean, we've been together, all of us, in bed. They never touch each other if they can possibly avoid it, even then. I've never intercepted a hot, longing look between them or caught them kissing or anything. I think it would be very hard for that kind of thing to be going on right under my nose and me not notice it."

Beanie didn't necessarily agree with her but also didn't press any more.

This time, when they met up at Clem's, though, it was one of the few times that they didn't spend dissecting one or the other of their relationships. Their mutual friend, Diana, was getting married and Beanie was the matron of honor, so she was planning the bachelorette party. It was going to be a weekend at Mohegan Sun, which was the closest casino to where they were all living. No one had to shell out to fly to Vegas or even get to Atlantic City. They were going to stay right at the hotel—despite the exorbitant prices for rooms— catch Louis C.K. at the Arena, drink way too much, gamble some, eat themselves into oblivion at the buffets and crawl up to their rooms when they were done.

That was all planned, and Maddie even had permission to go, which she was elated about. Mark and Matt tended to be somewhat overprotective of her sometimes. If it had been in town, or at least somewhere closer, she would have been more certain that they would let her go. But she was pleasantly surprised that it had taken relatively little cajoling on her part to talk them into it—although she knew that, if she screwed up big between now and then, she wouldn't be going anywhere.

But it wasn't the weekend at Mohegan that got Maddie into trouble with her guys. It was the get together that Beanie threw a couple weeks after that. It was almost an engagement party, but not quite. Lots of members of the wedding party and the bride's friends and family would be there, along with Beanie's and even some of Maddie's. She had gone unescorted—although with the full permission of the two of them. Matt had to work several double shifts in a row because one of the new hires in the squad kept calling in, and the shift needed to be covered. If there was no one else who wanted the work, then he was automatically elected to do it. Mark was away on business, due to arrive home late that night.

Of course, they had extracted promises from her to behave and not to drink too much, which she had an occasional tendency to do almost unintentionally because she was such a lightweight. But they made it very clear that they didn't want her driving home three sheets to the wind.

The first part of the evening had gone well. There were a lot of people there who Maddie knew besides Beanie and Diana, and she had spent most of the time answering questions about her current living situation—some of which were polite and curious, and others—the ones she ignored—bordered on the insulting, as did a few of the casual comments she heard from people on the fringes of the conversation.

At one point, Beanie drifted up to her, noting her tense face and putting her own drink into Maddie's free hand. "You look like you need this more than I do, sister."

When her friend drained the nearly full rocks glass in a few gulps, Beanie stopped and touched Maddie's shoulder. "Are you okay?"

Maddie nodded. "Yeah. I just need to learn to shut up about some of the choices I've made in my life, apparently."

"If they give you any hassle, you just tell them to go fuck themselves. You don't have to explain yourself to anyone."

"I know," Maddie sighed, but it wasn't until Bennie watched her friend slide onto the floor, her back to the wall, that she realized that Maddie was already seriously plastered, and she'd been dead wrong about which one of them needed the drink—and it certainly wasn't Maddie.

"You stay right there, honey," she said, reclaiming her glass. "I'm going to call Matt and Mark."

"No!" Maddie said with a bit more vehemence than her head could take. She stopped and took a deep breath, trying to will the spinning room to go away. "We don't need to bother them—besides, I don't think either of them is home yet. I drove myself here; I'll drive myself back." She tried to smile at her friend but knew it had come out something much more akin to a grimace. "Just give me a few minutes and I'll be good to go."

But Beanie wasn't going to have any of it and had stopped listening and stalked off to do exactly what she'd said she was going to. Maddie knew that—if she was able to get a hold of either of the guys—she was likely to be in some deep, deep trouble.

So, she got up, clumsily, barely able to stop herself from keeling over from dizziness at several points, and made her way outside, hoping the cool night air would have a sobering effect. She'd also snatched a couple big, buttery soft pretzels that she knew Beanie had made herself and began eating small pieces of them, until she realized that buttery was not the taste sensation she had thought it was going to be, according to her very unhappy stomach.

She wasn't out there for very long, standing very near the edge of the winterized pool with the big blue tarp over it, tears flowing freely down her cheeks before she heard an all too familiar voice calling for her.

Matt.

Maddie sighed, realizing that Beanie had called and probably awakened him. He'd had very little sleep in the past forty-eight hours, and yet here he was to collect her— although he sounded far from happy about it, making Maddie thing impulsively that she might not want to be found.

But it was soon much too late. He had already spotted her through the sliding glass doors at the end of Beanie's dining room, and her idea about running away from him flew out of her head immediately. That look—those piercing, pinning eyes—had her frozen in place instead, at least until he actually got out there, and she remembered just how big he was and, strangely, how much she loved him at the same time.

Matt walked to the same side of the pool, but slowly, as if he worried that she might try to jump in or fall in, his hand extended out in front of him. "I'm here to take you home, Maddie," he said calmly.

It only made him more worried when she covered her face in her hands and began to sob. He crept closer to her, praying she wouldn't lose her balance before he could get to her.

Genuinely concerned and hating to see her so unhappy, he asked, "Why the tears, babygirl?"

His empathetic, soft tone only made her weeping worse, which alarmed him. Even drunk, Maddie wasn't the maudlin type. She was generally a hoot when she was polluted, but something must've happened, although a quick glance back at Beanie, who was shrugging behind him, let him know that she had no idea what might be making Maddie so sad. Matt was determined to get to the bottom of it—probably through *her* bottom—but not until he had her safe in his arms.

The closer he got to her, though, the more she began to

back unsteadily away, which was exactly what he didn't want, of course.

Although he didn't like the way it sounded—and he knew that she would probably like it even less—he ordered in a no-nonsense voice, "Maddie, stay."

That halted her faltering retreat, but not until she'd knocked herself a bit off balance, just enough, in her inebriated state, to begin listing violently to one or the other side.

Matt's teeth clenched until they nearly broke, and he abruptly decided he was close enough—and she was preoccupied with trying to remain upright enough—that he could simply bend a bit and lower his shoulder at her, striding quickly and purposefully at her until he caught her right in the breadbasket, making her "oof" loudly as she lay over his back, safe in his arms, if inelegantly so.

But she couldn't be concerned, at the moment, about the ignominy of how he had picked her up. Instead, she began beating on his back with her fists, which, at first, he ignored.

Until she said with surprising sobriety, "Put me down, or I'm going to puke down your pants."

Since she was on safer ground and he was with her, he put her feet on the ground instantly, and she immediately began to heave onto Beanie's hedge as he held her head and stroked her hair, keeping it back and out of her way.

When she finally straightened up, he handed her a handkerchief, then took her gently into his arms. "Feeling better?"

Beanie appeared at his elbow with a glass of mouthwash, the dear, for which Maddie was eternally grateful.

"But why the tears?" Matt asked after she'd rinsed her mouth, tipping her chin up just a bit so that she couldn't avoid his eyes.

"Nothing. I just was drunk and let something someone said to me get to me when I shouldn't have."

She could see Matt's jaw clenching, and that wasn't a

good sign. "What did you hear?" he asked in a low voice that held a wealth of warning.

Maddie sighed, knowing he wasn't going to let go of it until she told him. "I was explaining to woman, who was curious and had asked, about our living arrangements. Someone who passed by at the time—and I'm not even sure I could recognize who it was—called me a slut."

As much as Matt desperately wanted to go back into the party and call whoever that bastard was out, he realized that Maddie's honor didn't really need defending against such idiots, and that his first duty was to make sure that she got home safely.

So, he swung her up into his arms, rather than over his shoulder, considering the unpleasant response that had inspired, and made his way back to the driveway with her.

Beanie helped him get her arranged in the passenger's side; she was already nearly asleep. He hugged Beanie and thanked her for all of her help, then drove the two of them home.

There, he reversed the process and carried her into bed. She had barely stirred the entire trip. He stripped her completely, throwing her clothes into the hamper, then tucked her into bed after awakening her just enough to give her an aspirin and a big glass of water to drink, then tugged her against him to fall asleep in his arms.

Unfortunately for Maddie, that was most definitely not the end of it.

The next morning, when she woke up and wandered out into the living room, hangover free, due to Matt's diligent efforts but still very drowsy, she found the two of them waiting for her as she traipsed through on her way to the kitchen.

"Good morning. I'd say sunshine, but you don't look very sunny this morning," Mark greeted drily.

She knew they weren't both there on the couch for nothing, but all she wanted in her life in that moment was a coffee. She was afraid that, if she didn't have one soon, she was going to run out of the energy necessary to make one, even though it was disgustingly easy with their Keurig.

Having already had several life-giving sips, she slowly wandered back to where they were both sitting, looking at her expectantly.

"What?" she asked, dropping onto the couch between them.

Matt snorted. "If you remember anything about last night, you can't possibly be serious with that question."

She hadn't really tried to think about the party, but when she tried to, she couldn't come up with much—a flash of talking to a group of people, something about pretzels and standing near a pool, which didn't make any sense because it was winter here. She could remember arriving, but only glimpses of things after that, really.

Mark reached out and squeezed her boot socks covered toe. "Needless to say, you're not going to be going out to any parties for the foreseeable future."

Maddie winced. "Was it that bad?"

"Beanie had to wake me up to come get you, and you were in tears over something someone said to you. And you puked in her hedge."

"Oy." She sighed heavily. "I'll have to call her and apologize." And before either of them could open their mouths about it, she turned to Matt and said, "I'm sorry you had to get up and come get me. I know you were totally wiped out by working all of those extra shifts."

Matt patted the hand she had laid on his thigh. "I sorry, too, Maddie, because you promised the both of us that you wouldn't get drunk, didn't you?"

"But I didn't mean to," she whined, knowing she wasn't

helping her cause in the least, because if there was one thing they both hated to hear from her, it was excuses. And although she almost always tried, very few of them were ever any good at getting her out of a punishment that they felt was due. And this one was going to be a doozey, she was sure.

Chapter 9

AND WHEN, after she'd had a real breakfast—complete with a slice of peanut butter toast and a small glass of orange juice, she realized that she had completely underestimated just how badly she'd screwed up.

She had a robe on—which was about the only clothing they allowed, and they only okayed that because the two of them ran hot, and they didn't want to keep the heat at the temperature that would have been necessary if they had insisted that she be naked all the time. Once Matt stood to bring her dishes back into the kitchen, Mark helped her up and disabused her of it in one easy motion, leaving her nude.

They stood with her between them, and she could literally feel the heat coming off their bodies as it bombarded her flesh.

"You know that we love you to distraction, Maddie, don't you?" Matt asked, turning her head towards him so that she could see the truth of that statement in his eyes.

"Yes."

Mark turned her head back to him, saying, "But you also

know that we won't hesitate to correct you when you've disobeyed us."

She swallowed hard but said, "Yes."

"Well, you promised us that you wouldn't drink too much. It was one of the reasons we let you go, besides the fact that we knew Beanie would look after you. And then I get there, and Beanie tells me that you were going to try to drive yourself home last night when you were practically too wasted to stand up."

"And very upset over what some jerk had said to you at the party, to boot," Matt added.

"I don't remember," Maddie pouted. "It's not right to discipline me over something I don't remember."

"The mere fact that you don't is reason enough," Matt growled.

"Right—if you had only had a drink or two, you wouldn't have forgotten what happened, now, would you?" Mark asked in his sternest tone, while guiding her into their room.

When they were all standing at the end of their bed, Mark turned her towards him and hugged her hard, then Matt did the same, before ordering, "Go get the A-frame out of your closet."

Her heart sank. It was going to be a bad one, but she nonetheless did as she was told, knowing that protesting her sentence would only make it worse. Much worse.

Once she'd set it up in the far corner of their room—which took a disgustingly short amount of time—she came back to stand between them again and was surprised to see that Mark had something in a long box that almost looked like the kind the bouquets of roses they often gave her would come in, but she was smart enough to know there weren't flowers in that box, no matter how pretty it looked.

And as much as she knew she probably really shouldn't

be, she was kind of curious about what was in it. It was a light blue box with a pretty pink ribbon, about eighteen inches long, and four inches wide,

He handed it to her, saying, "This is for you, although I know you don't want it. I bought two of them. Matt has his own, and since they're exactly the same, you only need to open this one."

Reluctant and excited at the same time—which seemed to her to be the story of her life with them—Maddie pulled slowly on the end of the ribbon, then opened the top of the box, staring into it with something akin to horror.

Its contents were the stuff that nightmares were made of —an old-fashioned, solid wood bath brush, with a long handle and an oval head that was probably about four by three inches or so. It looked horribly menacing, and it wasn't even in either of their hands—yet.

"Go put them on the hooks."

Some industrious person—Matt—had the brilliant idea of putting hooks in the corner in which she was often punished, so that the most common implements that were used on her hung there always, as a reminder to her to behave.

The both of them ended up there, but she was obviously not in any hurry to get them to their new homes, knowing that, shortly, they were going to be removed from their spots to be used on her backside.

When she returned, each of them kissed her gently, and then they each took a hand and guided her to the corner, positioning her over the sturdy wooden frame, each of them lashing down a wrist and an ankle.

"Are you comfortable?" Mark asked, and she knew that, conversely, he really was concerned that her position not cause her any undue pain.

She was going to be enduring enough of it in a moment, but in a very concentrated area.

"Y-yes, Sir."

"Good girl," he said, patting her bottom.

Of course, they didn't start out with the bath brush.

They began the way they usually did, with the flats of their hands against her immediately cringing behind. As far as Maddie was concerned, they really didn't need any other implements beyond their God given ones, but the guys insisted that—on certain occasions—nothing could beat one of their varied implements at getting their point across.

"Now, why do you think you find yourself here, Madeleine Hope?" Mark asked as unyielding palm after unyielding palm crashed into her bottom, leaving carmine red imprints wherever they landed.

Tears were already starting to flow, which wasn't unusual —unfortunately for her—even so early during a session, but she knew that wouldn't be considered any reason not to respond. "B-because I had t-too much to d-drink."

"Yes," Matt agreed, as he delivered a smack to her sweet spot, right where the curve of her butt met her upper thigh. "But it's more than that. Not only did you get drunk when you weren't supposed to, but Beanie told me that you were intent on driving yourself home. That you didn't want her to call us, either."

It was getting worse and worse. She swore off alcohol— in her head—immediately. She never wanted to find herself in this position again—especially once Mark reached for a bath brush, handing one to Matt, too.

Maddie immediately began to wail, knowing exactly what was coming next.

Mark laid the head of the brush on the cheek on his side, taking up nearly the whole of it, as he said, "You know, we're punishing you because we're selfish. We don't want to lose you—any part of you. And you know that you put yourself in danger by getting so plastered. What if Beanie hadn't found you and called us and you had just gotten into your car and tried to drive yourself home? Do you think you would have survived that trip?"

Some of the awful way she had felt that night—along with snatches of scenes of her conversation with Beanie and Matt—were coming back to her, and she had to admit—to herself—that he was very right. If she had gotten behind the wheel, there was no doubt in her mind that she would have ended up in an accident.

But that didn't mean she simply acquiesced to them and submitted to the punishment they had decreed she needed. The first smack of that bath brush down on her behind had her doing everything short of dislocating her limbs to try to get free, but that didn't stop the next she-didn't-know-how-many swats from raining down on her unprotected flesh.

His voice as hard and unyielding as the implement he wielded, Mark informed her sternly, "We intend that we'll never have to worry about you doing that again."

"I promise I won't drink ever again!" she almost screamed on a sob.

It was Matt who gently laid the tips of his fingers on her bare hip. "Too late, I'm afraid, Maddie."

And he wasn't kidding.

As far as Maddie was concerned, her punishment lasted several years. When they finally put the brushes down and helped her off the frame and onto their bed—on her stomach, of course—she had cried until her throat was raw from it and her voice was hoarse. Luckily, they didn't demand anything more from her. In fact, they both lay on the bed with her and rubbed her back, excruciatingly careful not to touch her ravaged bottom.

Although she should have anticipated it, she didn't. And

the next day, when it happened again, just before bed, it was a bajillion times worse, because her bottom was still nowhere near recovered from last night, and each crisp, hard swat landed on an area that was still very angry and mottled red, making it even more so.

That happened for three more days in a row—they each took time off of work to make sure that it did—and Maddie wasn't at all sure how she lived through it, frankly. The only thing that saved her was the fact that neither of them made love to her throughout it all, as if they wanted it to sink in, to have her contemplate the state of her backside and come to the conclusion that she should never disobey them, ever again—at least not about something that could easily have gotten her killed.

On that last night, when they lay her on the bed on her tummy, each of them came to her with a palm full of her favorite soothing lotion, which they rubbed into her beleaguered flesh generously and very carefully.

She knew they were concerned about her, mentally and physically—this was probably the worst punishment she'd ever received—or was it the time she'd driven her car without brakes? They were both bad, but she thought this one had lasted longer, although she couldn't be sure that wasn't just proximity—she still had the throbbing bottom from this most recent one.

And even then, neither of them made a move towards her except to comfort her. They were all three squeezed onto her queen-sized part of their enormous bed, with one of them rubbing her back and the other her rear end, and occasionally, they'd switch. It was so soothing that she couldn't keep from falling asleep, which she knew was their intention, but she had really wanted some time with the two of them, to kind of decompress from what had been happening for the past five nights, to talk about it and reassure them that she was okay, and even have them do the same for her.

But they seemed intent on helping her sleep, which her body was only too happy to comply with, and she was snoring softly in a matter of minutes.

The next morning, however, as careful as they were when they turned her over, there was no avoiding the pain of having her backside in contact with the sheets—even if they were seven hundred thread count Egyptian cotton.

But they weren't apologizing. Matt had begun suckling at a nipple that was—she couldn't imagine how—rock hard, despite the fact that her bottom felt like it wanted to fall off. And Mark had insinuated himself between her legs, latching his own mouth onto that warm, wet area between her legs and placing her legs over his shoulders, which put even more weight on the most uncomfortable part of her body.

They were both doing things that got her motor running, but, as usual, they were doing them for their own pleasure, not hers.

Hers, she found out later, would be a long time coming, as the last part of her punishment. But she didn't know that then. Every time they did this to her—which was most of the times they made love to her together—she hoped, usually in vain, that they weren't just teasing her. She never learned, and this time was no different from any of the others. The thing was that it wouldn't have mattered if she had known they weren't going to fulfill her today; her body responded of its own volition to what they did to her, regardless. She really didn't have any more control over it than she did over them—or her own life since she'd met them. Despite the fact that her bottom was throbbing in time with the tugging they were doing at her breast and between her legs, her body expected pleasure from them, and two thirds of it—two of the most sensitive places on her body—were getting it, and it just kind of expected that her natural conclusion would be reached.

Only to be sorely disappointed, night after night, morning after morning, for almost two months—until Matt could see that it was affecting her sleep.

They didn't tell her when they'd decided that she had their permission to come, but they made sure it was on a night when they would all be together. She had been severely restricted in other ways, too, for the past couple of months, and was only allowed to go out with one of them—not on her own. They had confiscated the keys to her car—even the spares. So, when she wanted to go anywhere, she not only had to get permission—which wasn't easy because of her misbehavior—but she also had to get one of them to drive her there. Not that she was allowed to go anywhere of any real interest, although, having been confined to the house so much for so long, even Walmart started looking pretty exotic pretty quickly.

They didn't make it into a special day or anything, because they didn't want her to feel rewarded. She had been on punishment, and that wasn't something that deserved a reward. So, as usual, she made their dinner that night—one of Mark's favorites, homemade spaghetti sauce with home-made meatballs, pasta, a salad and big slabs of garlic bread with cheese.

Dinner was—as it often was with them—loud and raucous. They were on differing sides on a lot of issues. Mark tended to lean towards the liberal side, which Maddie thought was unusual because she thought of him as the stricter of the two, although that was kind of splitting hairs because they were both pretty strict. Matt was much more conservative than his friend, and Maddie usually fell somewhere in between the two of them, philosophically as well as physically.

They all liked to have dinner as a time for just them, so the TV in the living room was off, but the stereo was on, playing mellow love songs that everyone knew. Maddie had even opened a nice red wine, although she didn't partake of it herself which the guys kidded her gently about, saying she was welcome to have *some* just not the entire *bottle*.

She gave them each a withering glance, then leaned back in her chair. "Hell, no! Henceforth, I am a confirmed teetotaler. And, for the record," she went on, "I didn't have an entire bottle of anything that night. I just had—apparently— way too much of something." They both laughed as she shifted uncomfortably in her chair, as if she still had to endure a bath brushing before being put to bed.

"Well, that's over, and you don't have to think about it anymore."

Matt waggled his eyebrows. "And your bottom is fully recovered." He would know—he'd been "inspecting" it at every possible opportunity.

Maddie pounced on that. "But it wasn't when you guys started to…you know."

How many years had they had together and she still blushed like a schoolgirl when discussing sexual matters among the three of them? They both found that very endearing and arousing. Now it was their turns to shift in their chairs.

When Luther Vandross' version of *Always and Forever* began, Mark got up and bowed in front of her, his hand extended. She went immediately into his arms, and they twirled around their big open dining area, which flowed into the big open kitchen and living room. Matt wasn't going to allow himself to be left out, of course, so about midway through, he cut in, very unapologetically. He wasn't as smooth a dancer as Mark, who had had been forced to take ballroom dancing lessons when he was a boy, but what he lacked in technique, he made up for in passion, spending the rest of his song with his hand splayed in the middle of her back and his head buried in her neck, almost beneath her hair, nibbling on her and delighting in the way she shivered in his arms.

"Hey! You two!! Get a room!" Mark called from his chair.

Matt stopped immediately, saying, "Great idea!" and proceeded to lead Maddie into their bedroom.

Mark followed eagerly, of course, and joined them where they stood at the end of the middle of their big bed. Because she had been out earlier in the afternoon, with Mark, to get the ingredients for dinner, Maddie was still in jeans and a pretty embroidered denim shirt.

"Stand still," Matt ordered, kissing her lightly on the lips as they proceeded to undress her.

They worked very well together when they were both concentrating on her, complimenting and exclaiming over each new part of her they discovered as if it was the first time, touching and teasing and adoring it when she sighed and caught her breath in reaction to their very delicate, almost reverent caresses. They didn't use the fact that there were two of them to hurry the process along at all, each taking his time exploring her body, as if they were trying to outdo each other in exciting her.

And Maddie ate up every bit of it. She adored being the center of their loving attentions, and every sincere compliment soothed her soul.

When she was nude, Matt picked her up and deposited her with infinite gentleness on her back on her bed and the two of them immediately joined her there, each of them trailing a set of big fingertips all the way up her body from the very tips of the toes on each foot, up over her tiny ankles, around the sides of her svelte calves and over the tops of her knees. Maddie began to writhe as they came closer to the area she most wanted them to touch, but they stayed their course and created lines of fire all the way up her thighs then onto her hips, not bothering in the least with the area between them, much to her frustration.

Two hands travelled up her sides, making her giggle because she was very ticklish, then up over her ribs to drag themselves deliberately over those already peaked nipples but not dwelling there in the least, slipping over her collarbone and down the inside of each arm to her palms, into which was pressed a warm, wet kiss, then starting again at her fingertips and trailing back up to the sides of her neck, the tips of two callused index fingers tracing the outline of her ears, then her jawline, up her blushing pink cheeks and into her hair, using it to hold her head still as they each bent to kiss her once, gently, on the lips.

Her hands had naturally reached out to rest on each of their broad backs, but when Matt noticed, he whispered throatily, "Put your hands on the headboard."

Maddie pouted as obviously as she could but was given no reprieve at all. In fact, they both stopped until she obeyed them, each reaching out to tweak a nipple hard for her reluctance. With her hands resting above her, she couldn't reach down to soothe that small insult, and neither of them did, either.

They were much too busy arranging her, with a leg over each of their hips spread wide open for them, but also making sure that she was still comfortable. They didn't want any cramping or aches and pains to detract from her pleasure.

As Mark reached his dominant left hand down to the area they had just exposed, cupping pretty much every inch of her privates with his big hand, Matt leaned down and kissed her deeply, his tongue delving boldly between her lips, sliding his hand into her hair, the side of his thumb rubbing gently over her cheek as he took her mouth with his.

Once he'd made his physical claim on her innermost self, Mark's hand was rarely still. And he didn't just go for the ultimate goal but explored every bit of her that was completely revealed to him because of her exposed position. His fingers played about her bottom hole, teasing, pressing slightly as if he was going to take her there, and smacking her bottom sharply when she tried to writhe away.

Matt ended their kiss to press his lips instead to her shell-like ear and growl, "*Submit*, Maddie." He wasn't entirely sure what Mark was doing, but he knew she shouldn't have been trying to get away from it, whatever it was.

Chapter 10

SOMETIMES, she just needed to be reminded, as if she needed their permission to submit to them, somehow. Matt's commanding words worked their magic on her, and they both saw her relax noticeably.

After he arranged himself between her legs, Mark's fingers encountered no resistance at all around her bottom hole, not that he spent much more time there. He had just wanted to remind her that they both possessed all of her, knowing that—although it was something she did enjoy, it wasn't something she found easy to acquiesce to.

From there, his fingers trailed up over her outer lips, tracing their outline, unable to avoid a very fleeting touch of his middle finger over the barest tip of her clit, which only made things much worse for Maddie for its ephemeral quality. She wasn't really even sure if he had touched her there, but her clit certainly knew, growing exponentially in hopes of catching more of it on his way back down, but it wasn't to be, which only made that bundle of nerves throb that much worse for the lack.

Instead, he split his index and middle fingers into a V

and tickled down the inside of her lips, outlining but not touching her straining bud until those fingertips found her deeper secret, closing and then entering her body much less gently than he had been stroking her before, pressing them forcefully up inside her till he could feel them bump up against her cervix and pausing there, very carefully manipulating that nerve filled part of her, watching her buck and writhe against his hand with a small grin.

Suddenly, though, with no warning that she noticed, they switched positions as smoothly as they could, so that it was Matt staring eagerly down between her legs and Mark who was kissing her as if he was never going to stop. But he didn't reach down and grab a breast, as either of them would sometimes do with his free hand. Instead, he flattened his hand and simply rubbed his palm against the barest tips of her peaks, making sure that was the only place—besides her lips—where he was touching her.

Maddie longed for him to take a breast in each hand, squeezing them against his mouth so that her nipples burst into his mouth to be suckled and licked incessantly.

But she was not in control of this situation, and so she had to endure being teased like that for as long as he enjoyed doing it, while, this time, it was Matt who was playing around her bottom hole. He was the less likely of the two to take her there, but he had learned from Mark to thoroughly enjoy pressing a finger or two inside her as she fought her own body's tendency to reject any invasion there and had to bend to his will.

But it wasn't until she felt him dab a bit of lube there that she began to moan in protest. It was Mark who whispered, "Submit," in her ear, just as Matt's index finger was beginning to make its way very slowly but deliberately inside her.

Matt could feel the way she was spasming around him, doing her best to follow Mark's instructions, but having only limited success in that, she hadn't tried to avoid him as she had Mark. But her body still automatically did its best to discourage him from venturing any further, not that he let that deter him in the least. Instead, he began to press harder and further, slowly, inexorably seating his finger within her as far as it would go.

But he wasn't happy just leaving it there. She'd soon become accustomed to it, and where would be the challenge in that? So, he immediately began to withdraw it again, then stationed his other fingers around as support as he began to invade her at will, popping in only enough to get past that clinging entrance and pulling out again, fucking her repeatedly with the tip of his finger.

Mark had to smile as he watched her begin to pant in response to what Matt was doing, although he knew that, if he asked her, she'd rail against it, but her body loved such attentions. Since she was having to work to breathe, he moved himself down a bit, so that her breasts were at mouth level, although that wasn't the first thing he did. Instead, he reached out and grasped them, squeezing from the base, watching how those tightened buds rose and listening carefully for the changes in breathing that he knew would result from his attentions, and he wasn't disappointed in the least. Between Matt and himself, and the fact that she'd had such a long buildup, she was more than ripe for the plucking.

And that was exactly what he started to do next, clamping his thumb and the bottom knuckle of his index finger over those tender bits and squeezing until she moaned long and low, not trying to writhe away, which always surprised him, but rather arching up, as if granting him further access to her breasts would somehow ease the ache he was creating in them.

But she was wrong. She knew she couldn't do anything to try to actively dislodge him, and so she had to endure, knowing that, as much as it hurt was at least as much as her body was quite thoroughly enjoying it.

Until Matt stopped repeatedly invading her with his finger and, instead, pressed something big and hard and not altogether unfamiliar against her flower, instead, and it wasn't until she began to feel herself being forced to stretch uncomfortably around it that she realized it was the plug that Mark used on her occasionally, to make sure that she never found it easy to accept.

And this time was no different from any of the rest. Matt advanced a little, then fell back, advanced a little and fell back, just like Mark did, stretching her open around the impossibly wide plug, although she thought he was doing it a bit more quickly than Mark usually did, giving her less time between advancements to become accustomed, requiring that she accept more of it each time than usual. She desperately wanted to reach down and stop him, but she knew better than to take her hands off the headboard.

All the way out and then all the way in again. This time, she knew it was very close to its widest point, and she prayed that he didn't force her to take all of it this time, but her prayer was not answered. He continued to push the chubby phallus until the meat of it disappeared inside her, making her cry out loudly once, then again when he pried it back out of her.

He continued to invade her, over and over again, until she had truly relaxed and accepted its presence, and only then, did he seat it fully within her, allowing her the relief of closing around its small neck, tucking it into her in a manner designed to make it hard for her to get rid of it on her own, leaving her feeling—still—almost uncomfortably filled down there.

Mark wasn't idle during this time, either—hardly. He had taken full control of her breasts, pinching and pulling and kneading them, twisting her nipples uncomfortably, then soothing them for a very short time with his lips and mouth, only to return much too quickly to more painful pursuits.

"Maddie!" Matt exclaimed as he pressed his fingers up inside her pussy. "You're sopping wet!"

"I know. She protests entirely too much, doesn't she?" Mark bit down, none too gently, on the heart of her nipple while flicking the other with his free hand.

"Definitely. It's as if you expect that we're going to allow you to come. Is that what you think, Maddie?" he asked, looking up at her.

Maddie felt as if she was being asked if she'd stopped beating her dog. Neither answer was going to be good, as far as she was concerned, but she went with the one that she thought seemed more submissive than the other. "N-no, Sir."

"Well, that's good. Because you should never assume that, babygirl," Mark said in a stern voice that just added another layer of excitement that, if they weren't going to fulfill her, she would just as soon have avoided. Not that she had a choice.

Now, it was Matt who produced a toy, one that they hadn't used very often on her—real wooden clothespins with rubberized tips. Maddie watched him plucking at her nipple, then saw him reach behind him on the bed to come back with one of those cruel things. She very nearly took her hands off the headboard in order to knock it out of his hand.

But she didn't. She swallowed hard when he grabbed hold of the end of her taut nipple, pulling it out and away from her body as much as he could, then letting the pin close on that sensitive nub. She began to keen as soon as he let go, but he was already on to positioning the other one, until she wore the both of them, standing straight out from her breasts.

That wasn't the end, though. Far from it. Mark didn't just

leave them be. Instead, he reached out and began to play with them, flicking the tips, tugging on each end, twisting and twirling them as they bit into her flesh.

And then he slapped her breast, very close to where the clothespins were clamping down, as if trying to dislodge them.

Maddie fairly howled with it, until Matt removed his finger from within her to replace them—rudely, roughly— with two more of them, pinning her legs back with his wide shoulders as he leaned into his possession of her most intimate parts, forcing her to spread herself around him in more ways than one and leaning forward to cup her clit with his mouth.

The explosive combination of pain and pleasure had Maddie wanting to scream and cry and come, all at the same time, but she was well aware that she hadn't been given permission to let herself go, although it was getting harder and harder to control her body's responses to what they were doing to it.

Matt knew exactly what she liked, and he employed every trick he knew about her preferences to make sure she was getting the most out of what he was doing. He suckled, licked, flicked and worried that little button of hers, all the while fucking her hard with his fingers, and—quickly— reaching down to turn on the vibration feature of the plug that was in her bottom.

Mark teased and tortured her breasts, kissing her deeply and whispering to her how good a submissive she was for them and how much they loved doing this to her.

"But you know that your pleasure is entirely in our hands —in more ways than one—don't you?"

Barely able to form a coherent thought, Maddie nonetheless answered breathlessly, "Yes, S-sir."

"Good girl."

The rare praise went right to the clit that Matt was busily mouthing.

"And right now, right this minute, you have our permission to come," he whispered, then took her mouth with his, keeping hers open beneath his as he reached down to tug the clothespins at the very ends, as if he was trying to pull them off her nipples without having to open them.

At the same time, Matt redoubled his efforts to please her, and he could feel the tension gathering inside her. She was clamping down on the fingers he had in her quim, as if she intended to break them off, and she knew that she was doing the same thing to the neck of the invader in her bottom. So, as he continued to love on her clit, he used his free hand to reach down and begin to pull the plug out— very slowly, deliberately dragging out the very intense sensations as long as he could.

When she came, Maddie found herself completely out of control. She screamed, she cried, she very nearly bucked the two of them—despite their size—right off her as they forced her only too eager body to several more completions. Eventually, all she could do was growl, deep and low in her throat, like a she-wolf, every muscle in her body tensed with ecstasy, fingers and toes curled, and if her hair hadn't already been curled, she was sure it would have been at that moment.

When they had deemed that she was through, the guys immediately set about trying to make her comfortable, removing the plug the rest of the way, stretching her legs out, and relieving her nipples from the grip of those tight clothespins, as they brought her arms down to rest beside her.

Maddie knew she should have been saying or doing something—thanking them profusely at least, but she just... couldn't. Intelligent speech—hell, any kind of speech—was beyond her right now, and they seemed to understand that, luckily.

After Matt arrived beside her with a warm, wet wash-cloth, cleaning her up intimately with a tenderness that brought tears to her eyes while Mark busied himself arranging the bedclothes the way he knew she liked, with the top sheet tucked in at the bottom—unlike the two of them—and her favorite blanket and comforter over them.

Each of them joined her, sliding up beside her on either side and holding her once they had gotten her and them-selves arranged, two big hands resting possessively on her belly, or stroking her hair back from her face, or gently rubbing her arm as she floated down from the top of the world.

Matt took her hand and kissed the back of it, lacing his fingers with hers. "We need to do more of that, I'm thinking."

"Which—pleasuring her, or making her wait for her pleasure?"

"Making her growl with it."

"I'm on board with that. But has she had her shots?"

Mark got a sharp swat on his bare belly for that. She was exhausted but not dead. Yet.

"Maybe we should do it again," Matt suggested specu-latively.

That had Maddie rolling onto her stomach in protest. She knew better than to tell either of them "no". Not that they allowed her to stay there long, though. She was almost immediately flipped right back over.

It was Mark who reached down to cup her kitty, sending sparks and shivers throughout her body as he did so, not that he noticed or would have let that stop him, even if he had.

"This is ours, isn't it?" he asked, slipping a finger between her folds to drag it over the top of her clit, making her muscles spasm involuntarily at his touch.

"Yes, Sir." She barely recognized her own hoarse voice.

"To do with as we please?"

"Yes, Sir," in a much smaller, but no less husky, voice.

"And if we decide that what would please us would be to do again what we just did to you?"

Maddie's eyes went wide, but she replied dutifully, "Yes, Sir."

"Good girl." He released her privates and kissed the end of her nose. "Why don't you get some sleep now? You must be exhausted."

And so, she was, practically before he'd finished his sentence.

Epilogue

IT WAS FALL, a time when Maddie became the closest to a sports widow as she ever got—baseball and football were on television twenty-four-seven, it seemed to her, and if the guys weren't watching it, they were talking or thinking about it.

She began—as she usually did about this time of year—to feel a bit abandoned. She was the center of their attention the rest of the year, and she didn't much like having her position usurped. But she was the dutiful wife to both of them, as always, making sure they had snacks and stuff to eat when they had friends over to watch the games with them, and even planning a—very private—Super Bowl party each year, with a menu of foods that had absolutely no nutritional value whatsoever but tasted great.

But once she'd brought them enough food to feed the army that they were and made sure the fridge was stocked with beer and soda, they essentially ignored her for two plus hours. Like a lot of women, watching sports wasn't particularly fulfilling for her. Oh, she would watch the occasional game with them, and she knew the basics of both sports. But it just wasn't her bag.

So, she had taken up the habit of going out with Beanie and her friends once she'd gotten them settled. They were okay with that—as long as she'd behaved herself lately—and didn't get into trouble.

That wasn't too hard to do. She and the girls sometimes went shopping, other times, they had dinner out. Occasionally, they just met at each other's houses to commiserate about being football/baseball widows and eat the same kinds of bad foods they'd all left for their husbands, but they watched a chick flick or two, instead, and all ended up crying together rather than screaming at the television or jumping up and down at a touchdown.

They ended up at Diana's new house, where she stuffed them full of homemade chili, corn dogs, and chocolate cotton candy. She was trying out her cooking skills—which were formidable—and her friends were only too happy to give her feedback about her most recent attempts.

Her den was big and open, with a large, comfy sectional in front of the biggest TV Maddie had ever seen. They watched some old classics—*The King and I* and *Casablanca*, as well as *Bridesmaids* and *Beaches*, which had everyone in tears.

But it was probably her fortieth screening of *Ghost* that left Maddie with such an ache in her heart for her men that she actually left the party to go back to be with them, as if it was suddenly brought home to her that every second she had with them was precious, even if it was spent watching sports.

They were surprised to see her home so early, having given her permission to stay overnight at Diana's, if she wanted to. The rest of the girls were, but she just couldn't bear to be apart from them one second longer.

When she arrived, they were each spread out in his own corner of their big couch, using the middle seat, where she usually sat, to hold only the essential snacks—garlic, parmesan, salt and pepper popcorn, Rold Gold pretzels, and spicy

Doritos. The dips were laid out on the coffee table in front of them, and she could tell that the queso/salsa/taco meat for their nachos was still simmering in the crock pot where she had left it.

She didn't hesitate one bit, once she got through the door, but raced up to Mark, who had just gotten up to build them some nachos and hugged him very tightly, unable to stop the tears that had been flowing freely down her cheeks since she left Diana's so abruptly. He hugged her casually at first, then more firmly as he realized she was crying.

"Baby, are you okay?" he whispered.

Matt had exceptional hearing—when he needed to—and that soft inquiry was enough to get him up and standing behind her, one hand rubbing her shoulder.

She turned around to hug him, too, practically sobbing by now.

Their game completely forgotten, they brought her to the couch with them, keeping her close between them. Matt gave the baseball announcer a nasty look before shutting the TV off completely and turning his attention back to her.

"What's the matter, Maddie? Do you feel okay?"

She nodded slowly, burying her face alternately against Mark's neck, then Matt's.

"Are you hurt?"

Another shake of those auburn curls.

"Did something happen between you and the girls?" They would have been as clueless as any other man as to what to do if she had said yes, but they had to ask.

"On the drive home?"

"No," she sobbed, not wanting to make them play a guessing game any longer. "I...we...we watched a really sad movie where the husband died and I just was missing you both too much to stay there. I had to come home and be with you, even if you were watching football."

"Baseball, now," Mark corrected, blushing when he realized that was a stupid thing to say. "Not that it matters," he finished lamely.

Matt stroked Maddie's hair. "Well, you're home with us now, and we're all safe and sound." They both pressed even closer to her, giving her a physical reassurance of their proximity. Matt even handed her the remote to the TV. "You put on whatever you want to watch, sweets, and we'll all watch it together."

Her selection of the latest episode of *Game of Thrones* surprised them. Not that they didn't like it, they did—all of them loved it—but it was hardly the most romantic of stories.

"Are you hungry?" Mark asked, and Maddie nodded.

"I didn't eat much at Diana's."

Mark frowned and got up. "How about if I build us a platter of your famous nachos?"

The program was paused until he came back with food and drinks for all of them, and then they settled down to watch their current favorite program.

About halfway through the episode, though, Matt found the remote and paused it, asking with a furrowed brow, "So you drove yourself home?"

Maddie, still somewhat distracted by the intricate story, nodded absently.

"And you got upset—you were crying—when you left Diana's?"

Maddie sat up a little straighter. She didn't like where this was going, but she knew better than to lie to them. "Yes," she admitted reluctantly.

"And what should you have done, instead?" Mark asked, turning her towards him.

"I should have called you to come pick me up, instead of driving home while I was so upset."

"Damned straight," Matt agreed.

Mark met his eyes over Maddie's head. "I think this needs to be dealt with. Pronto."

They stood, tugging her up and beginning to guide her into their bedroom.

"But what about Tyrion and Daenerys?" Maddie wailed.

"No buts, Maddie," Matt scolded.

"None but yours, anyway," Mark added with a wry smile as he closed the bedroom door behind them.

The End

Carolyn Faulkner

The words "spanking" and "discipline" have always sent a shiver up Carolyn Faulkner's spine. She knows she's not alone. Writing started as a way to explore her feelings. Soon short stories flowed from her pen featuring reluctant heroes taking the leading lady in hand, but always for her own good.

Today Carolyn is the author of dozens of books. She writes from her home in Maine, where she lives with her husband and leading man.

You can read an interview with Carolyn here:
http://www.blushingbooks.com/blog/?p=175

You may check out her website while it's under construction here:
http://www.carolynfaulkner.com

Don't miss these exciting titles by Carolyn Faulkner and Blushing Books!

Series books
Military Daddies
Lieutenant Daddy
Captain Daddy
Colonel Daddy
Major Daddy

Gentle Series

Her Gentle Giant
Her Gentle Cowboy
Her Gentle Soldier
Her Gentle Gangster
My Book
The Alpha's Woman series
The Alpha's Woman
Kosh's Omega
Red's Mate
An Omega's Awakening
The Omega Within
Mate of the Omega Collection

Adored series
Adored
Tessa's Wedding

The Red Petticoat Saloon series
Grading Garnet

Thornton Brothers trilogy
AJ's Hope
Beau's Desire
Cade's Wish
Thornton Brothers, Three-Book Set

Taken as His series
Prima
Tria

Priceless Love series
Priceless
Love's Possession
Dangerous Love

The Lark and The Bull
Doctor's Orders
A Babygirl for Christmas
Her Handyman
The Hart of the Matter
At His Hand
King of Hearts
True Desires
Lord Belden's Baggage
In His Care
Correct Me If I'm Wrong
Beauty Of The Beast
Tamed To His Hand
Daddy!
Amanda and the Stable Master
Lion
The Banished King
Northern Belle
The Cherished One
Forever Wife
Grace's Demon
Beauty's Beast
Captured by the Count
Male Order Bride
Sinful
Packed: The Enforcer
Submissive Love
A Heart Full of Heaven
Daddy's Girl
To Love a Man
Etta's Surrender
Her Secret Submission
Make Me
Let Me In

Tears of a Vampire, and Vlad's Story, Two-Book Set
Never Say Never
Under the Cover of Love
Her Guardian Don
Her Knight In Faded Denim
Forever In Love
Depths of Desire
The Power Of Love
Only Her
On the Razor's Edge of Paradise
Indiscreet
A Most Unsuitable Mate
Make Me Yours
Ready For Love
The Gentleman Dom
The Supplicant
Belonging
Hidden Desires
Her Bad Boy
All Is Right With the World
The Error Of Her Ways
At His Hand

Holiday Stories
A Holiday to Remember
Griff's Christmas Angel
A Season to Submit

Anthologies
Tamed By The Cowboy
Blushing Cheeks Vol. 1
12 Naughty Days of Christmas2017
12 Naughty Days of Christmas 2021
Dominating His Valentine

Blushing Books

Blushing Books is one of the oldest eBook publishers on the web. We've been running websites that publish spanking and BDSM related romance and erotica since 1999, and we have been selling eBooks since 2003. We hope you'll check out our hundreds of offerings at http://www.blushingbooks.com.

Blushing Books Newsletter

Please join the Blushing Books newsletter
to receive updates & special promotional offers.
You can also join by using your mobile phone:
Just text BLUSHING to 22828.

www.ingramcontent.com/pod-product-compliance
Lightning Source LLC
Chambersburg PA
CBHW030131260626
47156CB00008B/2894